Spies in Disguise

D1316155

Kate Scott was born in London. She has lived in Hong Kong, Paris, Scotland, and two tiny villages in France. She now lives in Dorset with her husband and two children.

Kate writes children's books, children's television shows, podcasts, and poetry. She's had lots of different jobs but now she makes up stories—the best job in the world.

She likes drawing, dancing, reading, and 1940s films. She hates raw tomatoes and being tickled.

Spies in Disguise

BOY IN A TUTU

KATE SCOTT

Sky Pony Press
New York

For Evie and Noah,
gadget inventors, storytellers,
and much loved members of the PHF

Sky Pony Press books may be purchased in bulk at special discounts for sales promotion, corporate gifts, fund-raising, or educational purposes. Special editions can also be created to specifications. For details, contact the Special Sales Department, Sky Pony Press, 307 West 36th Street, 11th Floor, New York, NY 10018 or info@ skyhorsepublishing.com.

Sky Pony® is a registered trademark of Skyhorse Publishing, Inc.®, a Delaware corporation.

Visit our website at www.skyponypress.com.

10 9 8 7 6 5 4 3 2 1

Library of Congress Cataloging-in-Publication Data is available on file.

Cover design by Simon Davis
Cover photo credit Clare Elsom

Print ISBN: 978-1-63450-695-3
Ebook ISBN: 978-1-63450-696-0

Printed in the United States of America

Chapter 1

I'm doomed. There's nowhere to go, nowhere to hide—I'm trapped like a rabbit in a cage.

She looms over me, her hands in plastic gloves. She's holding a bottle that has something foul-smelling in it. Any second now, that eye-watering gunk is going *on my head*. I lean as far back into the chair as I can go.

"For heaven's sake, Joe, keep still." My mom sighs.

"I'm trying!" I squeeze my eyes shut and focus on the one positive thing about this— no more wigs. My hair's finally grown enough to dye and style and there is no way a new hairstyle can  be as bad as the itchiness and worry that comes with wearing a long blond wig.

Probably.

When Mom and Dad first told me they were spies, I thought my life was about to be transformed into one long Best Day Ever. I thought it would be full of car chases and spy gadgets and missions to catch criminals. I thought I'd have a life like Dan McGuire, the hero of my favorite spy books. And, okay, it's true that Mom drives like a maniac and that we have a Mission Control hidden in the kitchen stuffed with top-secret gadgets. And it's true that Mom and Dad go around talking in code most of the time.

There's just one little problem.

When I say little, I mean ENORMOUS.

I've had to go undercover—as a *girl*.

Think about the most embarrassing moment in your life. Really think about it. The way your skin burns as if someone's shoved your face against a freshly filled hot-water bottle. The way your stomach decides to try to hide in your toes. The way you think about digging a large hole in a faraway place and leaving home to live in it. *That* kind of embarrassing moment.

The most embarrassing moment in your life is not even *close* to what I'm going through.

And there's absolutely no way I'd be doing it if it wasn't for two things:

1) We're in danger. Serious danger. Mom and Dad's last cover was blown and enemy spies are looking for a man, a woman, and their son. So me dressing as a girl helps keep the bad guys from finding us. And the girlier I look, the less likely it is I'll be suspected of being what I really am. That's what Mom and Dad seem to think, anyway.

2) Mom and Dad have agreed to train me as a proper spy, along with Sam, the girl who lives down the road from us and who's become my one real friend since we moved here.

After Sam and I managed to catch our teacher, Mr. Caulfield, trying to run off with a whole lot of school money, Mom and Dad *promised* that we could be in charge of an official, HQ-approved mission. Soon.

Except they've been saying "soon" for weeks. So as Mom puts the foul-smelling stuff in my hair, I bring up the subject—again.

"When are you going to find us a mission to take on?"

"Your problem is that you have no patience," Mom tells me, wrapping a wad of my hair in silver foil.

"Your problem is that you don't keep your promises," I say, scowling into the mirror in front of me. My head is covered in little rectangles of shiny silver foil. I look like an alien having a bad antenna day.

"If you want to be a professional spy, you have to have a professional attitude."

Mom wraps the last of my hair in the foil and puts the timer on.

"What's that supposed to mean?" My scalp tingles from the hair dye. I hope Mom knows what she's doing. She might be brilliant with high-tech gadgets and at changing her disguise at the drop of a wig, but I'm not convinced she knows a single thing about hairdressing.

"It means you have to be prepared to wait. Your dad and I want to find the perfect mission for you and Sam. Something we know you can handle."

"Something that isn't too dangerous, you mean." Mom's a top spy but she's also a mom—which means she worries about me getting into difficult situations. Though she doesn't seem to worry about all the difficult situations that dressing up as a girl has gotten me into. Like using the girls' bathroom, being forced to go to a pamper party, having to get changed with people who think discussions

5

about BRAS are a good idea. If you ask me, that's all a *lot* more dangerous and more worrying than a spy mission.

Forty minutes later, my hair's been rinsed and blasted with a blow dryer (noisy, hot, and *pointless*) and I'm staring at my reflection.

"I thought this was supposed to be an *improvement?*" My head is covered with bright yellow sticky-up tufts. I look like a hedgehog after a bleach-and-run accident.

"It is! Now you don't have to worry about that wig coming off every time you go to play soccer. And the styling is sweet. . . ." Mom fluffs the hedgehog spikes with her fingers.

I'm too traumatized to move. Somehow I imagined that the hair dye and styling Mom did would make me look a bit more like I was before— before I had to wear tights and a dress, that is. And yeah, it's great that I won't have to wear a wig any more—I *hated* that wig. I hated it the way Dan McGuire hates cockroaches in *Dan McGuire and the*

Six-Legged Invasion. But at least the wig was long and straight and could cover my face. This short, tufty hairstyle gives me nowhere to hide.

"All you need is a few of your nice hair clips and it'll be perfect," Mom says.

"Mom!"

Dad is the one who insists on me being a real girly girl—complete with pink, sparkly bunny hair clips and frilly dresses. I know now from Sam that not all girls dress like this or even like pink—something Dad doesn't seem to want to understand. But I thought Mom knew better.

"I know, sweetheart," she says. "But we do have to make sure your cover is completely convincing. The enemy spies are still after us, remember. It'll only take one slip for them to find us. . . ."

I sigh heavily. Obviously I won't do anything that puts us in danger, and obviously I've got the point that to protect us I have to dress up as a girl.

But it doesn't mean I have to be *happy* about it.

Sam comes over in the afternoon for a game of soccer. Sam's become my best friend since I started my new school as Josie, and we completed our own mission with the help of a few "borrowed" gadgets from Mom and Dad. She knows my parents are spies and she's promised to keep our secret safe. Mom and Dad must trust her as much as I do because even when we finally told them that she knew I wasn't really a girl, they didn't freak out nearly as much as I thought they would. They still insist Sam calls me Josie at all times, though, just to make sure she never slips up when we're not at home. So Sam raises her eyebrows at my hair and says, "Nice haircut, Josie," when Dad shows her into the living room. She waits until we go outside to react properly.

"Well, it's different." She catches my eye and snorts.

"It's a disaster. I look like a poodle that's had its fur ironed."

Sam laughs. "It's not *that* bad."

In Sam language, this means it's bad—very bad.

"Anyway," she says, grabbing my soccer ball from the lawn and spinning it on one finger, "I thought you were dying to get rid of your wig."

"I was." I run a hand through my hair and shudder. "I guess not having to worry about it falling off in a game is worth looking like a poodle."

Sam lobs the ball at me. "Come on, let's play. Take your mind off it."

Sam's the only person in the world who can make me feel better about my undercover disguise. She loves soccer as much as I do.

She likes the Dan McGuire books *almost* as much as I do. She sticks up for me when I'm in trouble. Most of all, she makes me forget that I'm a boy dressing up as a girl and wearing clothes that make me want to lose my lunch. Not to mention my breakfast, dinner, and assorted snacks.

I take the ball on my chest and drop it down to try a shot at the goal Mom and Dad set up at the beginning of the holidays. Sam manages to cover the whole length of the garden in about a second and slides in front of the ball before it passes the bar. She traps it with her foot and swings her right leg back to take the shot. I run up to block her but she's already slammed it into the net.

The downside of being friends with Sam is that she's a bit better at soccer than I am.

Yeah, all right—a *lot* better.

An hour later, after Sam's scored twenty goals and I've scored five, Dad appears at the back door and waves at us. "Hey, you two, come inside. We have some news."

He disappears before we can ask any questions. I glance at Sam, who's looking as excited as I feel. This must be it! Our mission has come in at last!

I run after Dad, Sam so close behind that we almost get stuck in the door.

Once we're in the kitchen, Dad sits down at the table next to Mom. There's a pile of papers in front of them. Dad grins at us, tapping the top sheet. "You're going to like this."

The word CLASSIFIED is stamped across the front page. Our first top-secret document—awesome!

"It's perfect." Mom leans over Dad's shoulder.

I pull out the umpteen sparkly kitten hair clips Dad made me put in my hair (he seems to think I need twice as many now that I don't wear a wig) and throw them on the table. *"What is it?!"*

Mom motions for us to sit down. I yank out a chair and plonk myself down in three seconds flat and Sam does the same.

"The community center is putting on an exhibition of soccer memorabilia," Dad says.

"Brilliant!" I'm already wondering if they have anything from my favorite team in the world, Santos.

"Hang on." Dad raises his hand. "HQ has discovered there is going to be an attempt to steal it—it's a really valuable collection. It's full of things that used to belong to the most famous soccer players in the world. The day after the exhibition finishes, there's going to be a large auction of sports memorabilia

in Spain. HQ thinks the thief will try to take everything there the night the exhibition ends. If they do it quickly, and fake the ownership papers, no one will realize everything is stolen until it's too late."

"Why don't they tell the police?" I ask.

"Their information hasn't come by routine channels and they can't go to the authorities without compromising their sources," Mom says.

Sometimes Mom and Dad go a bit heavy on the spy speak, but I get the gist. They can't tell the police about this because they might put their own spies in danger.

"Plus, they know enough to be sure it's *going* to happen, but not who's going to do it," Dad says. "There's no one to arrest yet."

"So they don't know who's planning the robbery?" Sam asks.

"No," Mom says. "But they think it's got to be someone from the community center staff. Some emails asking about the Spanish auction have been traced to the center's computer server—they just don't know who it was."

Dad flicks through the papers. "The community center has got CCTV security but HQ doesn't think it's enough. Their usual security spy teams are already on  other missions, so they've agreed to have the extra protection supplied by a less experienced team."

"You mean me and Sam?" I ask.

"That's right," Dad says. "You'll be our surveillance team. We need you to identify the thief so we can stop them before they get their hands on the memorabilia and take it to Spain."

Sam and I grin at each other. This is an operation worth waiting for!

"But remember, Josie," Mom says, "keeping your identity a secret should always come first. Nothing, not even this mission, is as important as that." Mom's wearing her most Serious Spy look, the one that means, "Don't even *think* about messing with me."

"I'm not very likely to forget my secret, am I?" I point at the pile of hair clips on the table. "So when do we start?" I can't wait to get a proper look at all the soccer stuff. Maybe they'll have some shirts from the Santos team. And maybe if we do a really good job they'll give us one of them as a reward.

A boy-girl can dream.

"The thing is, we have to give you a reason for being at the community center on a regular basis." Mom and Dad exchange a quick look and I get that sickly stomach feeling—the kind you get after eating too many gummy bears. The look they're giving each other is the sort that spells trouble. It's the type of look they gave each other just before telling me I was going to have to go undercover as a girl.

"What do you mean?"

"You can't just hang around the center all the time," Dad says. "That would look suspicious." He's using his come-on-now-be-reasonable tone of voice. It doesn't fool me for a second. "But now that the holidays have started, we can sign you up for one of their intensive courses, so you can spend lots of time in there without being questioned."

I narrow my eyes at them. "What kind of course?"

"Ballet lessons," Mom says quickly.

"Why do you always have to rush in like that?" Dad asks her grumpily.

"Because you don't say what needs to be said," Mom snaps back.

"EXCUSE ME!"

Mom and Dad stop glaring at each other and look sheepishly at me.

"*Why* does it have to be *BALLET*? Why can't we sign up for trampolining, or soccer, or tennis?!" It's as if my parents are *trying* to traumatize me.

Dad coughs. "Because it's been decided that ballet is the best cover for your activities. There's a two-week intensive course that finishes the day before the exhibition is moved on to its next location. It's a great excuse for spending a lot of time in the center so you can carry out your surveillance."

"But don't dancers wear *leotards*?" I can't believe Mom and Dad haven't spotted the obvious flaw in their plan. But everyone else will.

I hear Sam give a tiny snort next to me, which she quickly covers with a cough.

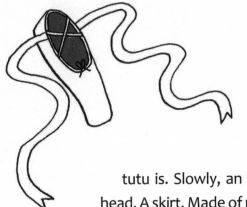

"Yes. That's why I've bought you a tutu," Mom says.

"A tutu?" I stare at Mom for a second while I try to remember what a tutu is. Slowly, an image comes into my head. A skirt. Made of material that looks like meringue. Usually pink.

Oh no, no, NO.

"It solves all the possible problems," Mom says cheerfully.

"A *tutu?*"

Sam snorts again. "Sorry," she says. "It's just..." She bends over, holding her hand to her mouth. She erupts into giggles.

I glare at her. "Ha. Ha. *Ha.*"

"You'll have to get one too, Sam," Mom says. "You should be dressed the same in case the other people in the class are only wearing leotards. If you're both wearing one it won't look so unusual."

Sam stops giggling. We make a face at each other—I know we're thinking the same thing.

Ballet lessons and *tutus*? This is NOT what we had in mind for a first mission.

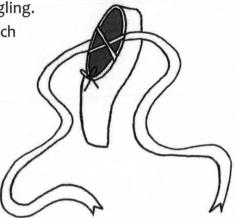

Chapter 2

If I could go back in time and tell my old self that he was going to leave his home, his school, and go on the run from enemy spies—and have to go under cover AS A GIRL—he would have laughed. But I'm not laughing now. Sam is, though. Loudly.

"I can't *wait* to see you in a tutu!"

We're up in my room with the file Mom and Dad gave us to go over, but Sam seems more interested in talking about my new disguise.

"You're going to be wearing one as well, you know," I remind her.

"Yes, but if I look at you, it'll take my mind off it. . . ." Sam dissolves into giggles again.

I scowl at her. The whole reason I liked Sam in the first place was that she didn't make fun of me the way my friend from my old life, Eddie, used to do. Sam is a better friend. Correction. Sam is *supposed* to be a better friend.

"Shouldn't we go through the mission file?" I wave it at her.

Sam gives one last hiccuping snort and nods, sitting up straight. "Yes. Sorry. I wasn't trying to be mean, but . . ."

" . . . you just couldn't help it," I finish for her.

She grins. "Sorry. Really. No more laughing." She pauses. "Except maybe just a tiny one when I see you in the tutu for the first time."

I ignore her and open the file. I want to be a proper spy more than anything, and doing well on this job is the first step to making sure that happens.

As I pull out the details about the soccer memorabilia, I remind myself of the reasons it's worth doing this:

1) The soccer memorabilia has to be protected—if it was stolen how could I look any soccer player in the face?

2) If we complete this mission, I'll be another step closer to being the kind of spy my parents are—being able to *do* missions instead of just reading about them in my Dan McGuire books. And instead of being the kind of spy whose disguise involves a collection of sequin-covered hair clips.

3) I improve my spy skills so that we stay out of danger from the enemy spies.

Besides, after the pink-dress-horror-fest Dad made me wear when I first became Josie, how bad can a tutu be?

I look over at Sam. She's still got a smile on her face.

Maybe I don't want to know.

The next day, my one comfort is that Sam and I have our first real spy training session before starting lessons in Tutu Torture. I can't wait.

Dad takes us into Mission Control, the secret room where Mom and Dad keep all their spy gear. It's my favorite room in the house, with its big blue screens on every wall, dozens of silver panels with buttons, slots, and receivers, plus shelves and shelves of gadgets. It's all a *lot* more interesting than the bathroom.

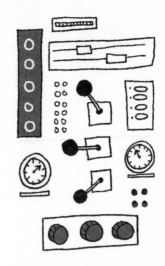

"First of all, we need to get you the proper equipment," Dad says. "The community center only has the usual CCTV cameras—a couple in reception and a few in the corridors."

"So you need us to add more cameras," I say.

"That's right." Dad reaches up to one of the shelves of gadgets and slides out a tray. On it are what look like clear, plastic eyeballs, and several packets of chewing gum.

So far, so weird, Dad. I pick up one of the eyeballs, run my fingers across it, and find a switch. When I

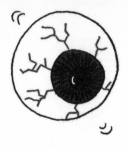

flick it, the eyeball leaves a bit of clear goo in my hand.

"I think your gadget just peed on me," I tell Dad.

"That's the glue—it makes this little camera stick to any surface."

"Right," I say, as the eyeball turns in my hand to look at me. "And it's motion sensitive."

"Exactly," Dad says. He grins at me. "You're a natural with the equipment, Josie. Must be in the genes." He holds another eyeball up to show Sam. "It's called the Eye Spy—it's the latest offering from HQ. It has an built-in sensor that alerts it to movement, triggering the filming function. The film is streamed here." Dad points to one of the screens on the walls of Mission Control. "We have software that analyzes the movement for suspicious behavior—someone lingering in one place, or tampering with the surroundings—so we're alerted to anything we should watch."

Sam takes one from the tray. "Clever."

"One-hundred-and-eighty-degree capability," says Dad. He strokes one of the camera eyeballs as if it's a puppy. Dad's a bit addicted to his gadgets. Not that I blame him. And it's a massive improvement on Dad's hobby in our old life. Let's face it—bait for fly fishing doesn't really stand up against plastic camera eyeballs that pee glue.

"And the chewing gum is for while you're waiting for something exciting to show up?" I pick up a pack and slip out a stick.

"No, Josie." Dad reaches out for the stick of gum. "It's a Tamper Tester." He unwraps the gum and holds it out. It looks like any other stick of gum except for a glint of silver in the middle of it. "Chew it for five seconds to activate it, then remove it and stick it to any surface you like. It monitors whatever it's stuck to and emits a signal that our software picks up. Just make sure you don't swallow it when you activate it," Dad says. "We had an incident with one agent in the field with this stuff."

"He didn't die, did he?" I ask.

"No," Dad says. "But the inside of his stomach set off a *lot* of alarms."

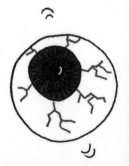

Dad scoops up some of the eyeballs and two packs of gum, and puts them into two small black bags. "After your first lesson, we'd like you to plant a few of these around the lobby, wherever they won't be noticed."

Dad gives us the bags then rubs his hands together. "Right," he says. "Time for spy training."

I grin at Sam. Finally!

Dad takes a small foldaway table from the side of the room and gets us to shut our eyes. When he tells us to open them again, there's a bunch of objects covering the table and he's holding a piece of blue cloth in his hand.

"Hey, is this the game where you cover everything with a tablecloth?" I ask. This is not what I imagined we'd be doing for spy training. I'm pretty sure Natasha Singh at my old school played this at her birthday party when we were about six. Mind you, maybe the experience will give me an edge.

"It's not a game, Josie, it's an exercise. Memory and attention to detail are vital skills for any spy," Dad says. "Right. You've got a minute and a half, to start you off slow."

A minute and a half—a slow start?!

I stare at the objects, repeating their names over and over in my head. I'm sure I'll remember everything but when Dad calls time and covers the table with the cloth, my mind goes blank. He hands over clipboards with paper and a pen, and Sam begins scribbling at top speed. I squeeze my eyes shut to bring up the image of the table—okay, I can do this.

Doctor Who sonic screwdriver, brown trilby hat, sheep-shaped hot-water bottle, brown toy dog, gray toy bunny, packet of fruit flakes . . .

I keep trying but nothing else comes. Maybe that's all of it? No, I'm sure there was more stuff than that. I open my eyes again and stare at the table, trying to see if I can figure out what's underneath the cloth by the shapes.

Next to me, Sam's still writing.

"Time's up!" Dad holds out his hand for our lists. Then he whips off the cover and checks each item we've written down. "Sam, good work—only one thing missed. Excellent. Josie, you missed quite a lot—you're going to need to practice to get your short-term memory up to speed."

"Okay, okay, I know." What I know is that Sam's done better than me on the test and I haven't. "Let's do it again."

Dad shakes his head. "Time for a different training test."

I clench my fists and focus. *This* time I'll do better.

Dad swivels round in his chair and presses a button on the wall. A keyboard slides out and he types in some commands. A second later, one of the screens on the wall shows a photo of a woman standing on a busy city street. "You have sixty seconds to examine this image," Dad says.

"Only sixty seconds?" I say in disbelief.

Dad beetles his eyebrows at me. "Yes, so don't waste time."

Sam's already staring at the screen. I quickly turn toward it. The woman looks a bit like a substitute teacher we had in fourth grade—what was her name? Miss Womble? Miss Wobble? Miss Wibble? Miss Wimple?

"Time's up!" Dad flicks a button and the image disappears.

Miss Warble, that was it!

Dad hands the clipboards back to us. "Now write down everything you can remember about what you just saw."

Oops.

Dad gives us ten minutes, which is a stupid way of doing things—he should have given us ten minutes to look at the picture and sixty seconds to write stuff down because what else is there to put except *Woman on a street*? Except maybe, *Looks a bit like Miss Warble from Bridleway Primary*.

When Dad's phone alarm bleeps, I've managed to add *Wearing a hat* and *Black hair* to my notes. But Sam's notes cover the whole page! Dad reaches out for both our clipboards. It's like being in school, waiting for a grade.

"This is excellent work, Sam," Dad says. "Really excellent. I'm impressed that you got the names of the shops. And only one letter wrong on the car license plate."

What car? What shops?

"Josie," Dad sighs. "I was hoping for a little better than this. Only two details?" He squints at the page—okay, so my handwriting isn't all that neat. "And that woman doesn't look anything like Miss Warble!"

Did Dad get taught by Miss Warble? I don't think so. But I decide not to argue.

Dad holds up Sam's clipboard. "Surveillance is about collecting detail. As much detail as possible. One tiny piece of information is sometimes the difference between a successful mission and one that fails."

"The names of the shops are important?" I don't get it.

"*Everything* is important," Dad says. "The shop could be a routine stop for the person in the picture—or it could be a meeting place. If it's a routine stop, then we start getting an idea of their everyday habits—and know when they break them. If it's a meeting place, then we can plant surveillance equipment and find out what they're up to. You can't afford to ignore *any* information."

"Even the color of their socks?" I grin at Dad.

"Everything," Dad says. "You never know what's going to turn out to be important."

Sam pokes me in the arm. "Being good with the gadgets is important."

"Thanks." I fiddle with another eyeball camera and make it wee on my hand again. Sam's right. Being able to handle the gadgets is *definitely* a good thing. Still, it would have been nice to beat Sam in one of the tests too. Especially now since Dad is telling Sam how good she was. Again.

Dad turns to me. "And don't worry, Josie. There are techniques you can use to remember things. For instance, if you need to remember to buy milk, you picture a cow."

A cow? What is my dad rambling on about?

"Look," Dad says. "Imagine you've got to go shopping, but you haven't got a pen or your phone for your list. You have to remember what you need in an inventive way. Say you want to buy milk, eggs, and a packet of peanuts. You picture a chicken sitting on a cow and the cow being chased by a squirrel because that image will stick in your mind."

Right, Dad, because a cow in a circus act is just what you need to think about when you go shopping.

"I get it," says Sam.

Of course she does.

"Thinking of a funny picture helps you remember what you need to," she goes on. "Cows give milk so it reminds you of milk, chickens lay eggs so that reminds you of eggs, and squirrels eat nuts so that reminds you of the nuts."

"Exactly." Dad holds his hands out. "And hey presto, you've got your list in your head."

"What if you need to buy cheese?" I say. "Do you think of a cow on top of another cow? Because the chicken and the squirrel are going to get hurt."

"You need to take this more seriously," Dad tells me.

"I *am!*"

But Dad decides that's enough for the first session and sends us off with some memory-training exercises to do.

Great—homework.

So far, spy training is like turning up at the fun fair and finding out that you've got to sell tickets behind the counter while everyone else goes on the ride. And the person next to you is a *lot* better at selling tickets.

Chapter 3

Before our surveillance mission can start, we have to go to the first session of Tutu Torture. On Sunday night I have a dream about being Dan McGuire in *Dan McGuire and the Scar of the Nile*, when he gets trapped on a tiny island surrounded by hungry crocodiles. Except in my dream, all the crocodiles are wearing tutus.

Sam and I arrive at the community center first thing on Monday morning so we can scout the place out and get changed without anyone realizing that Josie is really a Joe. There's a parking lot in front of the building and then two double doors leading into a large lobby where the exhibition is going to be set up. Several corridors run from reception to the sports hall, changing rooms, and studios, with stairs leading up to the offices and to the swimming pool.

After we've signed in for the course and got our membership cards, we head to the locker rooms. Luckily there's a single stall in the corner for people who prefer not to prance about in their underwear. I disappear into it while Sam stays outside and keeps watch. Once I've got the tights and leotard on, I pull out the tutu. It expands when the scrunched-up material hits the air, so standing in the cubicle with it is like being surrounded by cotton candy. I wrestle it to the floor, step into it, and pull it up around my waist. As I look down, I realize it's covered in thousands of small shiny sequins.

Oh fantastic. I'm a disco ball.

Mom told me this tutu was the only one left in the shop. No kidding. I'm surprised they didn't pay her to take it away.

"Are you ready yet?" Sam calls from outside the stall. "We should try not to be late for the first lesson."

"Promise not to laugh when you see me," I say as I stuff my clothes into my bag.

"I'm wearing one as well, remember," Sam says. "We're a team. A tutu team." She laughs.

I don't think Sam understands the difference between *her* wearing a tutu, and *me* wearing a tutu. "Just promise."

"Okay, okay."

I open the door. Sam looks like a girl in a tutu. It's a bit of a silly outfit, but it's not so bad. Maybe I look like her. Maybe I look all right.

Sam's mouth twitches.

"You promised," I warn her.

Sam whips around so she's not facing me and gives a strangled cough. Except we both know it's not a cough.

I walk over to the mirrors that line the wall next to the showers, take a deep breath and look.

It's . . .

I . . .

"NO!" I stumble backwards. "I can't do it!"

Sam reaches out and grabs my arm. "We have to, Josie. What about the exhibition? And what about completing a real spy mission?"

I point at my reflection—at the blond hedgehog with the disco ball a round its middle. "This is even worse than the first dress Dad put me in. And that was DISGUSTING!"

"Shhh," Sam says. "Remember why we're here. To keep an eye out for suspicious people. We can't do that if we're the ones acting suspiciously." She tugs on my arm. "Come on, we need to get to the class."

I take some deep long breaths, in, out, in, out—*I'm a disco ball! I'm a disco ball!*—in, out, in, out.

I remind myself I'm doing this to protect Mom and Dad, and to make sure I can be a proper spy.

"Let's go," I say, turning away from the mirror. "At least I won't have to see myself during the actual lesson."

"Um . . ." Sam says and then stops herself.

"What?"

"Nothing, come on." She hurries ahead, through the changing room door and down the hall to Studio Six, where the ballet class is. I ready myself for an hour of skipping about like a butterfly.

"I suppose I'm dressed for it," I mutter, as I follow Sam through the door.

I come in and see two things:

1) A woman in the middle of the room with bright red hair pulled up into a large round ball, like she's balancing a big tomato on top of her head.

2) A wall lined with mirrors.

And now the mirrors are reflecting two girls in tutus.

Us.

Sam—and a hedgehog/disco ball accident.

"I didn't want to tell you in case you freaked out, but dance studios usually have mirrors," Sam whispers.

Before I can get over the shock that I'm going to have to learn to dance in front of *mirrors*, the woman with the tomato hair glides over to us.

"I am Mrs. Rushka," she says. "You must be my new pupils." She looks us up and down. "Yes, you will need much work."

How does she know that? For all she knows, I might be an awesome butterfly.

"Your names?" Mrs. Rushka taps the top of our heads as if we're melons in a supermarket and she's checking to see if we're ripe.

I murmur my name and Sam does the same. This teacher isn't what I was expecting. I was thinking it would be some smiley woman in a floaty dress who would want us to pretend we have wings and fly around the room. This woman looks like she might ask us to do a military march.

"That is not the recommended ballet uniform for this class," she tells us.

Uh oh. All we need is for Tomato Head here to insist on us stripping off the tutus and my cover is up. I get a sudden rush of affection for my tutu—even the sequins—as I think about what would happen if I stood in front of the class in just my leotard and tights.

It wouldn't be pretty.

"Didn't you get the note?" Sam steps forward with her girly girl smile in place. She's very good at pretending to be a girly girl when it's necessary—a girly girl who's sweet and well behaved and definitely not carrying plastic eyeballs in her backpack.

"Note?"

"The note from our parents. They want us to wear tutus at all times."

Mrs. Rushka's lip curls. "And why is that?"

Yeah, *why*, Sam?

"They think it will help us be more professional if we're dressed like proper prima ballerinas," Sam says. She tilts her head to one side and sighs, as if her one true dream is to dance on stage.

I have to swallow a laugh since I know Sam's *real* dream is to play for England's women's football team in the Olympics one day.

Mrs. Rushka raises one eyebrow so that it goes almost all the way up to her hairline. It's pretty impressive, actually. "So you are both *serious* about ballet?"

Sam clasps her hands in front of her waist. "Oh yes!"

I'll have to tell her not to overdo it after the lesson.

Mrs. Rushka glances over at me and I force myself to give one small nod. Josie is supposed to be shy so I'm just keeping to my cover. But cover or no cover—*serious about ballet*?! Come on.

"Good," says Mrs. Rushka. "Then you will work hard. Very hard."

Great. Sam's just turned us into prima ballerina wannabes.

Mrs. Rushka sweeps off towards the mirrors and waves her hand at us to follow as several more girls come in to the studio. "Is this the intensive ballet class?" one of them calls out.

"Yes. And if you wish to be part of it I will expect you to be on time every day," Mrs. Rushka snaps.

The girl glances at the door, as if wondering if she should make a run for it.

I can't help missing the floaty teacher I'd imagined who was going to make us run around being butterflies.

Mrs. Rushka claps her hands so sharply it sounds like a firecracker. "Everyone to the barre, please, quick as you can!"

Bar? It's a nice thought, but we haven't done enough to be thirsty yet.

Sam pulls me by the arm over to a wooden rail by the wall. "This is the barre," she whispers.

What's a handrail got to do with dancing?

As we line up along the barre, Mrs. Rushka swoops along it, inspecting us. It reminds me of *Dan McGuire and the Army Attack*, when he has to go undercover as a soldier. I have to stop myself from saluting her.

"We will begin by learning the five positions of the feet," Mrs. Rushka announces.

Positions? Is this more like soccer than I thought?

The answer is no—ballet is nothing like soccer. Except that you're expected to move your feet a lot. But in soccer it makes sense— you're chasing a ball! You're trying to score goals!

But ballet is about bending your legs and arms in weird shapes and standing on one leg. A lot. It's a bit like training to be a flamingo. Actually, with my pink tutu, it's *exactly* like training to be a flamingo.

What Mrs. Rushka calls the warm-up goes on for about fifteen hours. She makes us point our feet and stick them in front of us, behind us, and to the side of us, over and over again. And all the names of the ballet moves are in French! So not only do I not know what I'm doing, I don't know what I'm doing in a language I don't understand.

First, second, and third positions are easy enough—it's just sticking your toes out and squatting. But fourth is harder and fifth position means putting your feet in opposite directions really close together. I wonder if the people who came up with Twister had anything to do with ballet. On my first go, I fall over. On my second go, the only reason I don't fall over is because I grab on to the barre. So *that's* why it's there!

Everyone else seems to be coping fine. Even Sam seems to have the hang of the whole holding-your-arms-out-as-if-you're-trying-to-hug-a-beach-ball move that Mrs. Rushka's showing us. I work even harder to keep up. I've got to look like I'm serious about ballet and, anyway, I don't want to stick out as the only one in the class who can't stay upright. My cover is supposed to be about staying in the background, not about giving a Josie-Falling-Over-On-Her-Bum Show.

Mrs. Rushka glides up and down, telling us to imagine that we have a wire coming out from the top of our heads, pulling our spine up towards the ceiling. I don't want to imagine anything like that! It makes me feel sick.

By the end of the barre work, my muscles have been taken out and replaced with red hot wires. I don't need an intensive ballet course; I need intensive care.

So much for ballet being easy.

During a break, one of the other girls comes up to me while Sam goes out to get us some water.

"Hi, I'm Ayesha," she says. She's wearing a white leotard and tights with a weird cardigan that only goes halfway down her stomach. Maybe it shrank in the wash. "Great class, isn't it?" she asks.

"Mmm," I say, pretending to be busy massaging my legs back to life, though actually I'm not pretending—I *am* trying to massage my legs back to life.

"I'm really looking forward to going *en pointe* once I get good enough," Ayesha goes on.

"What's that?"

Ayesha looks as though I've just told her I've never heard of the World Cup. "With pointe shoes."

I look at her blankly.

"You know, shoes with blocks in. So you can dance on the tips of your toes."

Blocks in your shoes? Who invented ballet anyway—aliens?

Then I realize that if you're in an intensive ballet class and are supposed to want to become

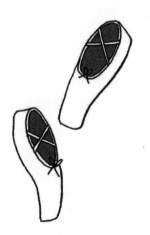

really, really good at ballet, then you should probably have heard of going *en pointe*.

"Oh yeah," I say. "Pointe shoes. Can't wait."

Ayesha goes on about *en pointe* for another ten minutes. I get more information than anyone in the world could possibly want about what it means. When you're good enough, you are given special shoes with wood in the tips so you can stand up on your toes to dance. Think about it—being on your toes with your whole weight bearing down on a hard wad of wood.

WHY WOULD ANYONE LOOK FORWARD TO THAT?!

Even though I try to put my Fascinated Face on, I guess Ayesha can tell I think the whole pointe business *has* no point because she moves away to the other girls. She's obviously hoping to find someone else who's looking forward to putting their feet through agonizing pain.

Good luck with that, Ayesha.

Sam comes back in just before the end of our break. She walks over and hands me a bottle of water. "I picked this up from the drinks machine in reception," she says in a low voice. "Looks like they're installing the exhibition there today."

Before I can reply, Mrs. Rushka does another firework clap to let us know it's time for the next round of Tutu Torture.

The thought of seeing the exhibition in place and being able to get on with the first part of our mission gives me the strength to stand up. Mrs. Rushka is pointing us to our places in front of the mirrors and gestures that Sam and I should go right to the front. I can't help flinching when I see my reflection.

Mrs. Rushka shouts out lots more French as she demonstrates new flamingo moves. Dad's right about his animal technique for remembering things, though. Thinking about flamingos is the only way I'm going to keep this stuff in my head. So when Mrs. Rushka shows us an *arabesque*, I picture a flamingo resting on one leg. When she demonstrates a *battement frappe*, I think of a flamingo batting away a fly from its foot. Then I use a beach ball to remember the arm positions. First position—hugging a small beach ball. Second position—hugging a big beach ball.

Third position—hugging a deflating beach ball. By the end of the session I've got them all, including fifth position—pretending you *are* a beach ball.

As we do all the flamingo and beach ball moves, Mrs. Rushka goes on and on about pointing your toes. Apparently if you don't point your toes, it's a complete ballet fail. If you ask me, ballet is a bit obsessed with toes.

Finally the lesson is over. Mrs. Rushka makes us all curtsy (weirder and weirder) and we're free to go.

Except that I can't seem to move my legs.

Sam and I agreed to wait until the others have gotten changed before going to the changing rooms, and it's just as well because my body is on strike. My arms and legs feel like all the bones and muscles have been removed, beaten with a big stick, and then put back. Sam's crumpled into a heap by the barre so I guess I'm not the only one. I walk—very s-l-o-w-l-y—over to her and give her a hand up.

"Ballet dancers must have really strong muscles," Sam groans.

"Too bad they have such bad taste in clothes," I say, watching as Ayesha disappears with the other girls, one of them wearing a neon pink leotard with purple flowers. It's the kind of outfit my dad would approve of. In other words, it's seven billion kinds of hideous. We walk carefully towards the door, trying not to let our legs realize that we're actually moving.

"I hope you enjoyed your first taste of serious ballet," Mrs. Rushka says.

"I loved it!" Sam says, giving her another girly girl smile.

"It is hard work, yes?" Mrs. Rushka says, holding open the door for us.

"Yes," I tell her. "It really is." For once, I don't have to put on an act.

As I stagger down the hallway with Sam, I even think about giving up spying. All I want now is a hot bath. Maybe a new pair of legs. And arms.

Then Sam hisses at me. "Look!"

At the end of the hallway, near the lobby, some men in overalls are bringing in boxes. Very large boxes.

"The memorabilia for the exhibition!" I forget that I can hardly move as I watch. Inside those boxes could be real treasure—the uniform of one of the most famous soccer players in the world, or one of the cups, or a soccer that was kicked by Pelé in a World Cup match. Now *that's* when toes are important.

All this awesome, beautiful stuff. And looking after it is completely up to us.

Chapter 4

Once we're dressed, we head out to the lobby area to plant the cameras and do an assessment of the kind of spy surveillance that the exhibit is going to need. It's time to begin Operation Eyeballs.

We check out all the CCTV cameras in the building by pretending to be hunting for a lost hair clip. I would actually love to lose mine, but Dad would just buy me ten more. I take the top floor and Sam takes the ground floor. Mom and Dad told us where to look for the red light that shows the camera's working.  When I check, they're all lit up. When we meet as arranged outside the girls' bathroom, Sam says it's the same downstairs.

"Maybe we should stick a Tamper Tester on one of the cameras in case the thief decides to mess with the CCTV. They might try to stop the robbery being captured on security footage," I say. "That way, Mom and Dad can monitor it."

"Good idea," Sam says.

I drag a plastic chair that's outside the sports hall and position it under the CCTV camera. While Sam keeps a look out, I quickly chew a Tamper Tester, leap up on the chair, and stick the gum to the underside of the camera.

"All set," I tell her, jumping down.

"We'd better get those eyeballs in place as soon as possible," Sam says.

"Let's go," I tell her. I can't help grinning as we walk down the hallway. Ballet in a tutu is as disgusting as a Brussels-sprout smoothie—but being part of a real spy mission is completely *fantastic*.

In reception, we sit in the chairs near the door, putting our bags down on the floor in front of us to make it look like we're just waiting to be picked up.

I unzip my backpack and pull out a bottle of water along with one of the Eye Spy cameras. I hand the water bottle to Sam, who unscrews the cap and then, according to plan, drops it on purpose.

"I've got it," I tell her. As I bend down to pick up the cap, I slip my hand under my chair, make the eyeball wee its glue and attach the gadget to the edge, where it will be able to film the lobby. As Dad promised, the camera sticks straightaway and can barely be seen.

A stream of people come in to book swim and gym sessions.

"Use them as cover," I whisper to Sam.

"I'll keep an eye out."

"Very funny," Sam whispers back, flashing me a quick grin.

Sam walks behind the people in line and quickly sneaks another eyeball camera onto the newspaper stand near the door. Then she wanders over to the rack on the wall with all the brochures about the community center's activities. She sticks an Eye Spy to the side of the rack with one hand as she flicks through the brochures with the other. She's about to head over to the central glass cabinet full of lifesavers and goggles, but I cough sharply and shake my head. The receptionist has dealt with everyone in the line and is peering over at us.

"Everything all right?" she calls. "Can I help you?"

"Oh, we're fine thanks!" I say, as Sam quickly hides the eyeball in her pocket and pretends to look interested in the swimming gear. "Just waiting to meet someone!"

The receptionist smiles. "All right then, sweetheart. Just give me a shout if I can help."

That's one of the worst things about being a girl: you get called names—horrific, horrible names, like *dear, love,* and *sweetheart.* I don't know how real girls put up with it!

A man in dark blue overalls wheels in a large glass cabinet and leaves it next to the stack of boxes.

"Someone could smash that easily," I whisper to Sam.

"Unless it's reinforced glass," Sam whispers back. "We should get another piece of that Tamper Tester on it."

"I'll do it," I tell her.

"Okay. I'll get an Eye Spy in place on that snack machine, then you take care of the reception desk when you've done the cabinet."

I feel a twinge of annoyance. Sam's acting like she's in charge of Operation Eyeballs. It's time to show we're equals. "Fine. And after that we'd better get out of here before the receptionist really does get suspicious."

I unwrap a stick of Tamper Tester gum and pop it in my mouth. I wander over to the glass cabinet. I cough the gum into my hand and casually lean against the case, quickly sticking the gum into one of the hinges.

I take out the last Eye Spy and approach the front desk. Up on the wall behind it is a large screen, showing promotional videos of all the activities the center offers. As I glance up, the film switches from showing a gym class to a swimming lesson. I flick the switch on the camera eyeball to release the glue as I put my hands on the lip of the desk and stick the eyeball underneath. The receptionist looks up and smiles.

"What can I do for you, dear?"

As she speaks to me, I notice a tall man in a tracksuit approaching the boxes of memorabilia and the glass cabinet. Did he see me plant the camera? I freeze, my heart playing the bongos in my chest.

"Are you all right?" The receptionist leans forward, peering into my face. "You look a bit pale, love."

"I'm fine," I tell her, my eyes still fixed on the man. But I can see now that he's not looking at me. He's leaning against the wall, watching as more boxes are brought in.

I sigh with relief and turn back to the receptionist who gives me an encouraging smile.

"Did you want to book a session?"

Uh-oh—I should have thought of something before I walked up to the desk! "Um, I wanted to ask about swimming."

As soon as it's out, I realize I shouldn't have said it. The screen showing the swimming lesson must have put it in my head. Pretending to be a girl means I can't ever go near a pool. I used to love swimming before all this, but as Josie I'm supposed to be allergic to chlorine and have a fear of open water. I'm supposed to make sure I never, EVER go near a bathing suit.

"Lessons? Pool opening times? Swim team?" the receptionist asks. As I think of what to say, I glance over at the tall man—he's still looking at the boxes and the glass cabinet where everything will be displayed. Why is he so interested in that cabinet?

"The swim team." Again, it just slips out, probably because I'm distracted by the tall man. Swim meets are what I used to do in my old life, when I was Joe, not Josie.

"Oh well, then, you want to speak to Mr. Jones." The receptionist smiles and points at the man in the tracksuit. "He's our head swim instructor." She leans over the desk towards me. "He's only been here a little while and he's set up so much—he's amazing!"

"Really, he's new?" I look over at Mr. Jones again. My internal spy alarm rings. *Maybe* he came to work at the community center so he could carry out the robbery. Could I have found our threat on the first day?

"Yes. Only been here a couple of weeks and done more than the previous instructor did in two years," the receptionist says. She waves over at the man. "Mr. Jones! This young lady is interested in joining your swimming team!"

Mr. Jones is walking over. I need an excuse, quick! I think fast. If I'm going to investigate him then I'll have to pretend to be interested in taking part in a meet. It doesn't mean I actually have to *do* it. I take a breath. As long as I manage this right, there's no reason I'll put my cover at risk.

"Josie? Mom's just texted to say she's been held up and we should catch the bus home." Sam comes up next to me. She's obviously heard our conversation and decided I need help. There's no time to explain. I see Mr. Jones give another backward look at the memorabilia boxes. A new employee who just *happens* to be right in the lobby as the soccer memorabilia is delivered and is obviously dying to see what's in the collection? He's got to be high on our Possible Thief list.

"We've still got time," I tell Sam. Wouldn't it be great if I was right to suspect Mr. Jones? I'd be a bit ahead of Sam for once!

"So, you're interested in joining the swimming team, are you?" Mr. Jones asks. He smiles down at me. I have to crane my neck to look up at him. It's a good thing I'm not wearing a wig any more because at this angle it might have fallen off. He rubs his chin. "Have you got any experience?"

"Uh, yeah. I used to swim for my school team before we moved."

Mr. Jones takes another step closer, still smiling. His teeth are very white and straight. He could be in a toothpaste commercial. "Oh, did you move here recently?"

"Yes."

"I see . . ." He looks at me intently for a moment, then he blinks and is back to flashing his I've-never-eaten-any-sugar-in-my-life smile. "So which school did you swim for before you came here? Because the thing is, we could really use some strong swimmers for our team," Mr. Jones says. I see his eyes flick over to the moving men as they sort the boxes. He could definitely be a suspect. I've got to keep playing along.

"I'm a strong swimmer, I just haven't competed for a while," I tell him, ignoring the question about my old school.

Next to me, Sam coughs. The cough isn't a covering-up-a-laugh cough, though. It's a what-are-you-*doing*? cough.

I ignore her. Sometimes, when you're a spy, you have to take risks. Like in *Dan McGuire and the Mountain of Doom*, when he had to chase an enemy spy down a mountain on a snowmobile.

"Great." Mr. Jones taps one of his gleaming teeth. "Well, um . . . ?"

"Josie."

Mr. Jones flashes me another smile. "Okay, Josie. I've got to go and teach a lesson in a minute but bring in your suit and come and find me in my office tomorrow. We'll do tryouts in the pool and then I'll give you the forms for joining the team."

Tryouts! I can't do that! My secret would be out faster than you could say bikini bottoms! I hear Sam take a sharp breath beside me but I manage to keep my expression calm.

"Right," I say.

"Excellent. See you tomorrow." He nods at Sam. "Do you want to join the swimming team too?"

"No, thanks," she says, shooting me a look. "I'm already busy doing *other* activities."

When Mr. Jones has walked away, Sam grabs my arm and pulls me towards the exit.

Once we're outside, Sam turns on me. "What are you doing, signing up for the *swim* team and agreeing to do a tryout?!"

I don't like the way she's making out that my talking to Mr. Jones was a huge mistake—even if it kind of was, at least at the start. Now it looks like it was a stroke of luck—I've

got a way to investigate a prime suspect! "I think he could be the thief," I say. "The receptionist says he's only been at the community  center for a couple of weeks so it could be a cover. It's a really good one, if you think about it."

"That's great, but *your* cover says you don't swim. For a good reason—*remember*?" Sam looks at me as if I've lost my mind.

"The time trial's no problem. I'll just pretend to forget my suit. I can keep coming up with excuses while we investigate him," I tell her. "Anyway, we're not at school so my cover can be a bit different here," I say, knowing that Mom and Dad probably wouldn't see it that way. They're always telling me that one cover is hard enough to maintain without creating another identity to try to remember.

"You still can't go swimming, though, can you? Not without giving it away that you're not a girl," Sam says, lowering her voice.

I start walking towards the bus stop so that Sam has to follow. "I know *that*. But I told you, I'm not going to follow it through, am I? I'm just going to plant some surveillance gadgets in his office so we can see what he's up to."

Sam stops and spins around towards me. "Why didn't you talk to me about it first? We're supposed to be a team."

"I had to act quickly!" I say. "Besides, you're the one who was telling me what to do in the lobby— you didn't talk that over with me first."

Sam's eyes widen in shock. "That's completely different!"

I rush on. "Anyway, it's not like we can't have our own ideas, even if we are working together."

Sam shakes her head. "I just think it could lead to trouble."

We walk to the bus stop without saying anything more. I feel like a balloon that's had the air let out of it. I thought Sam would be impressed with my having spotted Mr. Jones as a suspect but instead she's treating me as if I've done something wrong.

There's only one thing to do about it.

I'm going to have to prove I'm right.

Chapter 5

The next morning, I can't believe how much my legs hurt. Sometimes I've felt a bit achy after a soccer game but it's never been like this. This must be how Dan McGuire felt in *Dan McGuire and the Mystery Marathon* when he had to run four races in a row as part of a spying mission during the Olympics.

"Come on, Josie, up you get," Mom says, yanking the curtains apart.

"It's supposed to be the holidays," I tell her. "You know, a *holiday*? When you don't have to get up early?"

"Yes. And you're in an intensive ballet course, remember?" Mom pulls out my tutu from the closet where I'd stuffed it and lays it on the chair with the leotard, tights, and my dress for the day. "Besides, Dad and I want to give you and Sam a training lesson before you go. So up and at 'em."

My old everyday mom was good at nagging. Shame my new spy mom is as well.

Mom pauses by the door. "Oh yes, we've just heard from HQ about your mission."

"They're not canceling it, are they?" I sit up in bed and throw back the covers. Was HQ impressed by what we did in Operation Eyeballs?

"No, of course not," Mom says. "HQ is very pleased. That Tamper Tester you put on the CCTV showed that some of the cameras have been damaged—that was good thinking. They've just got some new instructions for you. But I'll tell you about them later—when you're dressed." She throws me a get-up-*now* look and leaves.

I let out a sigh of relief. I'd hate to be pulled off the mission just when it's going so well. I look at the dress Mom's laid out for me. I can tell Dad bought it—it's covered with a pattern of tiny pink strawberries. He seems to think that girly girls really love fruit. As I pull it on, I can't help fantasizing about catching Mr. Jones on my own, and Mom and Dad and HQ being so delighted with me that they insist that I become a professional spy immediately—and go back to being Joe . . . in *pants*.

After breakfast, Sam comes over and Mom tells us we're going to do our spy training in the car as she and Dad have got an errand to run.

"It's best to sit as far back in your seat as you can," I whisper to Sam.

"What?" Sam looks confused. She won't in a minute.

Sure enough, as soon as Mom hits the highway, she puts her foot down. She speeds past everything—even the fast sports cars that are trying to show off.

My mom can outrun them all.

This is the part about having spy parents I really like.

Sam flattens herself against her seat. "I see what you mean now," she says. Then she breaks into a grin. "This is *great!*"

We smile at each other as Mom presses down harder on the gas pedal, turning the grass by the highway into a streak of blurry green.

"What you've got to remember," Mom calls back to us, "is that you can put a whole mission in trouble by talking about it. So you must learn how to say one thing and mean another."

"Like when you said you and Dad needed to run an errand—but you really meant you have a spy job to do?"

"That's right, Josie," Dad says. "You've got it in one." He brings up the secret control panels on the car dashboard and I see the screen that's showing our progress with the little red blinking dot. A green dot appears close behind us on the screen.

"Are we being followed again?" My stomach drops like a lift going to the ground floor. I remember when we first left our old house and were chased by enemy spies—a little dot behind us meant danger. Big danger.

"No, don't worry. That's a friend," Dad says. "We're about to say a quick hello."

"Just remember, you two," Mom adds, laughing, "don't try this at home."

What is she talking about now?

Then Sam points at the screen and I see. The green dot is drawing level with our car. I look out the window and see a silver car with dark windows next to us. I know Dad said it's a friend but what if he's wrong? You can't see inside with those windows. What if it's a trick? How can they tell? My breath catches in my throat as if I've swallowed a sweet the wrong way.

Now Dad's speaking into his phone—though he's not saying words, he's saying numbers. "Sixteen, eleven, two thousand, six," he murmurs. "Three, five, two thousand, three." It must be code for something.

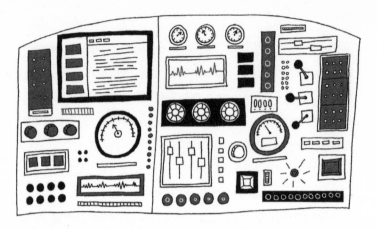

"Ready?" Mom grips the steering wheel carefully and checks the rearview mirror.

I glance at Sam—she's holding on to her seat belt so tightly that her knuckles have turned white.

"Ready," Dad says.

We're completely level with the other car now. I see the tinted window come down as Dad's window also whirrs and lowers. Something small suddenly flies into the car.

"Dad!"

"It's fine, Josie," Dad calls, holding up his fist. He's clutching whatever it is that just came in from the other car. "Successful delivery."

As Dad's window slides back up, Mom speeds forward and outruns the silver car. In a few minutes she's signaling and slipping into the middle lane and then taking the next exit.

"So that was a drop?" asks Sam.

"That's right," Dad says. "Some codes we've been asked to break. You're not the only ones with a mission, you know."

"If you can pull it off, a moving drop is safer than a fixed location. It lowers the chances of witnesses," Mom tells us.

Dad turns round to us and grins. "As long as you're a quick catch."

"And if you have a skilled driver." Mom winks at us in the rearview mirror.

Dad laughs. "You just like the excuse to get on the highway, Zelia."

Mom takes one hand off the wheel to prod Dad in the arm. "Yeah, well, *you* can't resist any new gadget from the HQ catalog."

"True," Dad says.

I look over at Sam who's grinning her head off as she takes it all in. I lean back into my seat, feeling a smile spread across my face. Okay, so having to dress up as a girl is horrifying and horrendous, but sometimes my parents being spies is definitely, completely GREAT.

We're driving at a normal speed down a smaller road now. Mom signals as she prepares to take the next turn. "As part of your training, we need to develop some code phrases," she says. "So we can give each other messages to do with spy business but make sure they won't mean anything to anyone else."

"So," Dad says, " 'We're having hamburgers for dinner' means you're going to have a spy training session."

"And 'You girls have a lot of homework to do' tells you we have an update on your mission from HQ," Mom says.

"You should think about developing some that you can use at school too," Dad says. "Or when you're on a mission and you need to let each other know if you're in danger."

"I know!" Sam says. "We can use phrases that we use at school anyway—you know, like 'Boring' or 'Got a pencil?'—things we say to each other all the time. We can make them mean what we need them to. Like 'Boring' for 'Danger.'"

"That's an excellent idea, Sam," Dad says. "You really are a natural at this."

"Yeah, well done," I say. It *is* a good idea—so why couldn't I have had it? Sometimes it feels like Sam's better at everything than I am.

Sometimes that's a bit annoying.

Mom takes a long route back from the drop to make sure we're not being followed so we have the rest of our "hamburgers for dinner" training session in the car. Dad digs around in a large black briefcase at his feet and passes us a pile of code phrases to learn later. It turns out that when Mom said "You girls have a lot of homework to do," she didn't just mean it in the code sense. Unfortunately.

"So your new brief from HQ is to copy the community center's CCTV security footage from the last few weeks," says Dad. "It's all backed up on a hard drive, so if we have it, we should be able to see who meddled with the cameras."

"Because whoever broke the CCTV cameras is probably the same person who's planning to steal the soccer memorabilia," Mom adds.

"Right," I say. I bet Mr. Jones is going to be on that film—I can't wait to get hold of it.

"The server and backup might be in the main office," Dad says. "Just stick one of these on the hard drive and it will copy every piece of data on it." He hands back what looks like two long black tails and Sam and I each take one.

"What *is* this?" I bend the tail so that it curls round my hand. It feels like it's made of rubber-coated wire.

"The Copycat Clone." Dad shifts in his seat so that he's facing me. His eyes are lit up—he really does love his gadgets. "Compatible with any drive, it copies the data and stores it in its tail."

"Clever," Sam says, sticking her Copycat Clone tail in her bag.

"It really is," Dad agrees.

"Your other instruction is to map out the community center—every single entry and exit point," Mom says.

"Why?" Wandering around the center with a notepad and pencil does *not* sound like a proper spy job.

Mom accelerates to pass another car. "It's essential to know your surroundings in any operation. And for this mission, we need to see how the thief might plan an escape with the memorabilia. Jed, can you give them the 3D Wands?"

"Delighted to." Dad rummages around in the briefcase again. "Here we are—the 3D Wand—the ultimate in measurement gear." He pulls out two shiny rods and hands them back to us. "Looks like a pen but the laser technology calculates distances, cubic volume, everything. Just click and shoot at every wall around you and it will scan and store the information needed to create a 3D image of the center."

I click at one side of the car and then the other. A blue light runs along the length of the Wand. Moments later, the reading flashes up on the tiny digital display in red lights.

Sam examines hers. "Brilliant. We could use it at school to plan escape routes from lessons."

"I don't think so, Sam," Mom laughs.

"We also want you to try to get one of these attached to anyone you suspect," Dad says. He holds up something that looks like a tiny black button.

"What's that?" I reach out for it. It's almost as thin as paper and has what look like silver threads running through it.

"It's a GPS tracking device," Dad says. "If you plant one on someone, you'll be able to tell where they are at all times using the Sniffer Dog app we've downloaded on your phones. It'll show us if anyone is hanging around the exhibition or if they go anywhere unusual." Dad gives us a handful each to put into our backpacks.

I know exactly who I want to get a tracking device attached to but I don't say anything. Since Sam thinks I'm risking my cover by showing an interest in swimming, I don't want to bring Mr. Jones up with Mom and Dad until I'm sure I'm right. I'm starting to really like the idea of beating Sam to finding out who is planning to steal the exhibit. I want to show Mom and Dad that I'm just as much of a natural at being a spy as she is.

Mom takes another turn and I realize that we're coming up to the community center. Her phone bleeps as she pulls up in the front parking lot. "Time to go, you two. Don't lose those gadgets." She checks her phone and turns to Dad. "It's a Code Amber—we'd better do a track in and red ten."

I love it when Mom and Dad speak spy. They sound like characters in my Dan McGuire books.

"Don't forget your hair clip, Josie," Dad says as I open the car door.

And then they go and spoil it.

Chapter 6

I've been hoping that maybe yesterday's ballet lesson was just extra hard because I'd never done it before. As we warm up, my arms and legs don't feel quite as bad as they did this morning. Maybe today will be easier.

Ten minutes later I realize how wrong I was.

Mrs. Rushka is even stricter than yesterday and she won't shut up about the wire-through-the-head thing. "Keep your spine straight! Your head up, up, up! If you want to be serious about ballet, you must work very, very hard," she tells Sam and me. "Now that I know you are both serious, I will push you hard."

I *knew* Sam had gone over the top with the whole "We want to be professional" routine.

The sooner I prove Mr. Jones is the thief by finding that CCTV footage, the sooner I'll be able to take off this tutu for good. I keep thinking how great it will be when I show Mom and Dad how brilliant I am at spying. And how Sam will realize it was worth changing my cover story.

"Josie! I wish you to show us your barre work now." Mrs. Rushka sweeps up to me, interrupting my thoughts.

Twenty grand pliés later—that's a big squat with toes turned out—and my muscles have all remembered that they HURT. A LOT.

After Mrs. Rushka has made some rude comments about me needing to tuck in my bum more, she makes us do some really fast footwork with—surprise, surprise—pointed toes. You have to push out your foot really fast and sharply over and over—snip, snip, snip. I feel like a pair of scissors. Eventually even Mrs. Rushka can see that we're all about to collapse so, as a break, she sits us down in front of some ballet film clips.

At first, I'm not really concentrating, but I can't help noticing how the dancers are doing all the things we've been learning *perfectly*. Now that I've been trying to do it myself, I know how hard all that prancing about really is. I've got to admit it—it looks pretty cool. The men lift the women above their heads and make it look like they're lifting a bag of feathers. There's no way I could lift Sam and make her look like a bag of feathers. And all of them are like one long muscle—they've got to be some of the strongest people in the world! At one point, a male ballet dancer crosses the stage in one leap. He's like a deer with its tail on fire. That move would be handy on the soccer field—you could get right past an aggressive tackler.

"Soon, you too will dance this beautifully," Mrs. Rushka tells us.

In your dreams, Mrs. Rushka.

After the lesson, Sam and I pretend to need a drink of water so that we can go into the locker room after everyone else has left. The other girls seem to have gotten the hint that we don't want to make friends, and keep their distance—though maybe it's just that they don't want to hang out with the hedgehog-disco-ball girl.

"You keep a lookout; I'll knock on the door to the main office," Sam says. "If no one answers, I'll go in and look for the security footage hard drive."

"We'd better come up with a code phrase in case someone comes along and I need to let you know," I say. "And we need an excuse for you being in the office if someone gets by me."

"I could say I was looking for the lost and found box," Sam says. "I could have lost my watch."

"Okay," I say. "So if someone comes along, I'll call, 'I think I see where you dropped it,' and you'll know to get out of there."

Sam grins. "Operation Copycat is underway."

When we get to the main office, Sam knocks and peeks in. It's empty. She darts inside and I stand guard in front of the door, pretending I'm checking my phone. But a second later, a door down the hall opens and a guy in overalls comes out with a mop bucket. He's heading towards me—and the office!

Uh oh.

There's no way that Sam will have found out if the hard drive is there yet, let alone copied the footage—she needs more time! I decide to go off plan and try something else. "Excuse me?"

The man stops as his hand's reaching out for the door. "Yeah?"

"I was just up by the swimming pool. Someone's spilled a carton of strawberry milk in the viewing gallery. It looked like it might be dangerous—you know, people could slip on it."

The man sighs heavily. "And might this 'someone' have been you?"

"No! It was a little kid. I just thought you'd want to know," I say, doing my best Very Concerned Citizen impression.

The man raises his eyebrows but nods and walks off in the direction of the stairs. "Yeah. Thanks."

Some people are so ungrateful. It *could* have been true.

The man's just rounding the corner when Sam opens the office door.

"Wait, he hasn't gone yet," I hiss.

She pulls back into the room for a second until the coast is clear and I wave her out again.

"You were supposed to warn me if someone was coming—that was the whole point of coming up with a spy code phrase," she says.

"You'd only just got in there," I say. "We wouldn't have been able to come back for ages, so I made the most of us being here now. Anyway, it worked, I got rid of him."

"But it might not have worked!" Sam walks away from the door and gestures for me to follow her. When we're a few feet away, she turns to face me. "You keep taking risks."

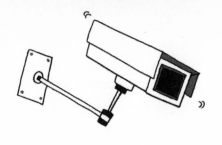

"It's a mission, that's what you have to do," I say.

I just gained her some extra time to look for the hard drive and she's complaining! "Anyway, did you find it?"

Sam shakes her head. "No—I looked everywhere but it's obviously not where they keep the hard drive for the CCTV after all. Let's get on with the mapping for now and have a look for it again tomorrow."

"Right. I'll go upstairs and you start down here," I say.

"You're going to see Mr. Jones, aren't you?"

"I've got to tell him I can't do the tryout."

Sam frowns. "And you'll tell him you can't be on the swim team too?"

"Yeah, sure. As soon as I've put a tracking device on him."

"Okay, but still—make sure you tell him you can't join the team. I'm worried you'll get caught somehow," Sam says.

Sam is getting seriously bossy. Doesn't she realize that real spies take risks? Where would Dan

McGuire get if he never did anything dangerous? And it's not like I don't know I can't get in a swimming pool when I'm supposed to be a girl! But there's no time to argue.

"I'll meet you in reception," I tell her.

Sam nods and heads off down the hallway while I go upstairs. A couple of people are chatting by the door to the pool and I duck into an alcove until they pass.

As soon as they've gone, I take out my 3D Wand and click and shoot the nearest walls.

In the next hall, I have to hide behind a pillar next to the staff toilets while another group of people go by. Eventually, I manage to shoot every surface with the Wand.

I tiptoe over to the area where the offices are—though it's a lot harder to walk quietly in the pretty-pretty girly shoes I'm wearing. Dad doesn't seem to understand that sneakers are essential spy footwear.

One of the office doors has a sign on the front: *Swim Instructor*. The door is slightly ajar but I can't see anyone through the opening. I double back up and down the corridor to make sure I haven't been followed. There's no one around. I nudge the door open with my foot and pop my head in. "Hello?"

The room's empty, but Mr. Jones can't be far because he's left his cell phone on the desk and his jacket is hung over the chair. I snatch up the phone and slip the tracking device inside the back of it like Dad showed me. I've just snapped the cover in place when I hear a voice behind me.

"Hello, Josie."

I'm so startled I nearly drop the phone. How did he appear without me hearing him? Luckily I had my back to him so I don't think he could have seen what I was doing.

"I'm sorry, I was just looking at your phone," I say. "I've always wanted one like this." I quickly put it back on the desk.

"Just as long as you weren't planning to run off with it." Mr. Jones laughs to show he's joking but I feel my cheeks go red. He's the thief, not me!

"I just came to tell you I can't do the tryouts. My mom says she doesn't want me to go swimming for a while because I'm still getting over a cold." I cough into my hand and then sniff a bit to make it extra convincing.

"Oh dear, what a shame." Mr. Jones peers into my face. "Are you *sure* you're not up it?"

I force myself to cough again. "No, sorry. But maybe I could take those forms you were talking about," I say. "In case I do join the team." It's never going to happen but Mr. Jones doesn't need to know that until I've proved he's the one who's planning the robbery.

"How can you resist joining, Josie?" Mr. Jones gives me a smile that reminds me of a shark. "After all, you swam for your school where you used to live, right?"

"Um, yeah, that's right," I say.

"Where was that again?" Mr. Jones smiles in an I'm-such-an-idiot-for-forgetting way.

This is definitely *not* where the conversation should be going. I've got to get out of here!

"Sorry, but could I just get those forms? I'm in a bit of a rush." I sling my bag over my shoulder and take a step towards the door.

"Sure, sure, no problem." Mr. Jones walks over to his desk and opens a drawer. He rifles through a pile of papers. "Here you are." He hands over a wad of forms. "Just make sure you fill them out in full with your address, phone number, previous address, swimming certificates, and so on."

I scan the forms—it's more like a passport application than an I-want-to-be-on-the-swim-team form. At my old school, all you needed to give was your name, address, and doctor's details. I can't give my previous address—that's top secret!

"You see, for the big meet, which I hope you'll be taking part in, obviously we need proof that everyone on the team is as good as they say they are. If you're not able to do a tryout before the meet, we'll need those certificates. You see, there was someone here last year who lied about their experience. It was very disappointing. I had to kick them off the team." Mr. Jones shakes his head sadly. "So that's why we need the swimming certificates or tryouts to prove that everyone on the team is up to standard."

Excellent! He's provided me with a perfect excuse not to join the team! "I don't know whether we've still got my certificates. They might have got lost when we moved," I tell him. "But I'll look." I'll just make sure I never find them.

I make a move to leave but Mr. Jones holds up his hand. "Hang on, Josie."

I glance behind me at the hall—I have to suppress the urge to make a run for it. There's something about Mr. Jones's toothpaste-commercial smile that really makes me nervous.

"Don't worry too much about supplying all the information. Just make sure you give me your previous address and I can figure out where I can look up the certificates." His white teeth gleam down at me. "I've got my ways of tracking things down; don't you worry."

For some reason, the way he says this makes my stomach flip like a pancake. I shake the feeling off and force myself to smile back. "Okay, great," I tell him. "See you later."

I run down toward the lobby, thinking of the little tracking device safely stored in his phone.

We've got our ways of tracking things down too, Mr. Jones. Don't you worry.

Chapter 7

Sam's made friends with the receptionist and is chatting away to her about all the different activities that the center runs. I guess she's developing a source—a spy contact who helps you collect information—like Dan McGuire in *Dan McGuire and the Seven Secrets* when he gets a journalist to identify an enemy spy. I feel a little annoyed. She complains about me taking risks but *she* keeps trying to run the mission.

I bet she's just jealous of me having spotted the most likely suspect first.

I walk up to where the soccer memorabilia is on display. It's the first time I've been able to get a proper look.

It's fantastic! I forget everything as I take in what's there. There's a ticket from the 1966 World Cup final. There's a jersey that belonged to George Best. There's even a Santos shirt signed by Pelé! For a second I dream of stealing the memorabilia myself. That shirt would look awesome on my wall. Well, it would if my wall wasn't pink.

"Amazing, isn't it?" says a voice behind me.

I jump and turn round to see Mr. Jones. He's sneaked up on me *again*. What's he doing here? I can't help feeling he's followed me deliberately.

"Yeah, it's great," I say.

Then I realize, he's not following me—he's come to look at the exhibition. He must still be working out his plan to steal it.

"Weren't you in a hurry, Josie?"

"Oh, yeah. Well, I'm just waiting for my friend to finish . . ." I look round and see that Sam isn't talking to the receptionist any more. She's sitting on one of the chairs, staring at us.

Mr. Jones glances over, looking amused. "I think your friend's waiting for you."

"I'd better go," I say, taking a last look at the exhibit and stepping away.

"Don't forget, I'm counting on you to take part in the swim meet," Mr. Jones calls after me, as I walk over to Sam.

I wave to show I've heard and then jerk my head to the door. "Let's go."

Sam jumps to her feet and we hurry out.

"I thought you were going to tell him you couldn't do it?" she says as soon as we're outside.

"I have to pretend to take the forms home to Mom and Dad first," I say. "I can't say no without an excuse."

Sam takes the forms I'm still holding in my hand and flicks through them. "Why does he want so much information? I've never seen a joining form like this."

"Apparently they get swimmers making up how experienced they are," I say. "Mr. Jones said it happened here last year and he had to disqualify someone."

"I thought you said he's only been here two weeks?"

"Yeah, good point, he has. . . ." It's even more proof that he's not who he says he is! I'm one hundred percent sure now that Mr. Jones is the person who's planning to steal the memorabilia. "I've put a tracking device on him so at least we can keep an eye on where he goes. But I'd like to search his office too, and maybe plant an Eye Spy." I take out my phone and tap the Sniffer Dog app logo—a picture of a dog sniffing the ground. Sure enough, the little red marker on the screen map shows that Mr. Jones hasn't moved.

"We shouldn't narrow it down just to him, though," Sam says. "Remember, we don't have any proof yet."

"Apart from him changing his story about how long he's been here and hanging around the exhibition all the time, you mean." I hold up my phone for her to see Mr. Jones's dot on the screen. Sam was like this when we were investigating Mr. Caulfield at school. She didn't even think *he* was guilty at first and I was right then too.

"I'm not saying it isn't suspicious," Sam says, "but we should look at the other staff as well. I found out quite a lot from the receptionist. We can rule out the yoga teacher—she's going on retreat tomorrow and won't be back until after the exhibition's finished. And two of the other staff members are leaving for their vacations in the next few days. But the two janitors have access to the whole building and a good excuse for being there a lot. And the receptionist was going on about how the memorabilia must be worth a fortune and she wishes she had some money to go on vacation like everyone else. We should spend some time on them too. We haven't even checked out Mrs. Rushka yet."

"Okay, but we don't have time to mess around, you know."

"We don't have time to get it wrong, either," Sam snaps. "Until we've got evidence, we should look at *everyone*."

Luckily the bus pulls up and ends the conversation. Why can't she just trust me? Maybe the whole idea of us being a spy team wasn't such a great idea after all.

At home, we give Mom our 3D Wands and an update. Mom's really happy about Sam's receptionist spy source and goes on for about a million hours about how smart Sam's been to narrow our suspect list down so much. I turn away so she doesn't see me scowl. My parents seem to think Sam is perfect.

Finally we get on to the hard drive and the mapping we've done.

"It's a shame the hard drive wasn't in the office but maybe our map will help us figure out where to look next," Mom says. "Wait until you see this." She pops the Wands into a slot in the wall and presses some buttons. The Wands flash blue light as the information uploads. Mom flicks a final switch and a 3D model of the community center comes up on a screen. It spins around so that we see all the entrances and exits in the building.

"That's fantastic!" Sam leans in to take a closer look.

"Awesome." I really do see why Dad loves his gadgets so much.

"Wouldn't the basement be a good place for the hard drive to be kept?" Sam points at the plan. "Machines are often kept somewhere where the temperature is low, aren't they?"

"Excellent thinking, Sam!" Mom says. "That does seem a likely place for the CCTV server and backup to be kept. See if you can get down there

tomorrow." Mom beams at Sam. "It's great that you're thinking like a spy."

Yeah. Great.

Mom gives us some more Eye Spy cameras to put near each entrance and exit so that we can track who's coming and going. "So far, we haven't picked up any major suspicious activity from the reception area, so whoever is planning the theft is being careful."

"Hasn't it shown people hanging around the exhibition a lot?" Why haven't they noticed Mr. Jones being there all the time?

Mom laughs. "It's an exhibition of soccer memorabilia, Josie. People *are* going to look at it! We've seen plenty of people standing around admiring the exhibition. This bit of film is typical."

She walks over to one of the panels and flicks a switch. A screen flickers and then comes into focus, showing four or five people standing in front of the glass case, peering into it. She flicks the screen off again.

"But isn't it suspicious if the same person does it a lot?"

"Well, yes," Mom says. "But we'd need more evidence than that to be sure."

I pretend not to see the told-you-so look on Sam's face.

More and more it feels like we're not working together. She doesn't like my ideas, and these days it feels like she always wants to be in charge. I'm beginning to understand why Dan McGuire works alone.

Chapter 8

We're walking down the hallway on our way to ballet on Wednesday morning when I hear a familiar squeal.

"Josie! Sam!"

It's Melissa, the girl from school who forced me to go to her birthday pamper party. And of course she's with Nerida and Suzy. They're always together at school, so I guess during the break they meet up too—like a pack of wild animals, but sparklier.

I look down at my glittery tutu. Great. Just what I needed. The girly girl gang witnessing my Tutu Torture shame.

"You've had your hair done!" Melissa reaches out to touch it and I flinch away from her. When you've been wearing a wig for a while, it's hard to get out of the habit of keeping people as FAR AWAY from your hair as you can.

Melissa's staring at me so I fake a smile. "I wanted a bit of a change."

Because everyone wants to look like a hedgehog now and then.

Melissa beams at me. "It's gorgeous! And I love your clip!"

I remember the sparkly elephant hair clip that Dad made me put in my tufts this morning. Dad's not just obsessed with his spy gadgets, he's also obsessed with my hair accessories. Apparently he thinks sparkly clips are what separates girls from boys.

"You're taking ballet lessons?" Nerida tilts her head and smiles. "Wouldn't have thought you and Sam would be into it, to be honest. I thought

you two were all about soccer."

"What, it's not possible to like more than one thing, Nerida?" Sam faces her with her hands on her hips. "And anyway, didn't you know that a lot of professional soccer players take ballet to improve their footwork and develop stronger muscles?" At least Sam hasn't forgotten how to stick up for me, even if she prefers bossing me about these days.

"No . . . I mean, of course I knew that," Nerida says.

Liar, liar, your bra's on fire.

"I *love* your tutu," Melissa tells me.

"It's so sweet! Especially with your hair."

Sweet is not a look I am trying for. Ever.

"Thanks," I say. Can we just go now?

"Come on, Josie, we're going to be late," Sam says.

We hurry down the corridor and push through the doors to Studio Six. Safe.

Sort of.

Mrs. Rushka hurries over to us as soon as we come through the door. "Josie! Sam! Come in, come in." Mrs. Rushka looks the happiest I've ever seen her. Her tomato hair is quivering with excitement.

She does her firework clap and everyone comes to attention. "Girls! I have an announcement to make. We're going to put on a show so that all my talented pupils can be seen!"

I don't like the sound of this.

"Which day will it be?" Ayesha is smiling so hard her face might crack. "I can't wait to tell my mom."

"The evening of the last day of the course," Mrs. Rushka tells Ayesha.

That's the last day of the soccer exhibition. That's the day it's most vulnerable to getting stolen—because the Spanish sports auction is the next night. If the thief acts quickly enough, they'll get the stuff sold off before anyone can stop them. So if we stop coming to the lessons to avoid being in the show we'll have no reason to be here all the time. But if we're in the show, how can we look after the memorabilia? And how can I avoid having to dance like a flamingo in PUBLIC?

"There is no time for proper auditions, so I have drawn up a cast list," says Mrs. Rushka. "I will put it up on the door at the end of today's lesson as I don't want you all to be distracted. Now, more than ever, you need to work hard."

Maybe it won't be so bad. Maybe I'll just be in the background and can do a few hug-a-beach-ball moves. Maybe being in the show will actually make it easier to keep an eye on the exhibition—we can nip out between scenes and check on it.

But when we all crowd round the notice that Mrs. Rushka puts up at the end of the lesson, there it is—a nightmare in a swirly handwriting:

```
Princess Delia – Josie

Prince Caspian – Sam
```

I don't take in the other names on the list because all I need to know is there at the top. I'm the leading lady and Sam is the leading man. I stare at my name in horror—it might as well be written in blood. I thought dressing up as a girl was bad enough. But dressing up AS A PRINCESS? AND DANCING LIKE A FLAMINGO?

NOOOOOOOOOOOOOOOOOOOOOOOOOOOOOOOOOOOOOOO!

"Ah, I see you're surprised," Mrs. Rushka says. "I knew you'd be pleased." She taps the top of my head. "You have worked very hard, Josie—you have excellent stamina and strength. Your pirouettes are progressing nicely."

She's talking about my flamingo spins—I don't want my flamingo spins to be progressing nicely! I was working hard so I didn't stand out, not so that I could be picked to be a pirouetting princess!

I glare at Sam who's still staring at the cast list in shock. This is all her fault. If she hadn't forced us to pretend to be serious about ballet, this would never have happened.

Not that anyone else is happy either. One girl called Jeannie keeps giving me evil looks as if I *asked* to be cast as the lead. You can see she thinks I've stolen her chance to be discovered as a star in the making. Like appearing in a dance show at the local community center is a one-way ticket to the next *X Factor*.

Dream on, Jeannie.

Sam and I have a conference in the locker room. Sam doesn't even let me open my mouth before she starts.

"Your mom and dad said we shouldn't do *anything* to risk your cover," she says. "I don't think you should be drawing attention to yourself by going on stage. And it's bound to involve quick costume changes. That makes it way too dangerous. You've got to tell Mrs. Rushka you can't do it."

There she goes again, bossing me about! It's not as if I don't know all this. And Sam's not the one in danger of having her boy parts exposed. *I'm* the one putting the mission first. Again.

"We can't give up our reason for being here—we'll never catch who's trying to steal the memorabilia. Besides, the show is the night when HQ thinks the thief will make his move. It works in our favor to be here," I say. I've had enough time to think about it. It's going to be a complete nightmare, but if Dan McGuire can run across a factory floor covered in broken light bulbs (*Dan McGuire and the Light Legend*), then I can get up on stage and do my beach ball arms.

"I know, but —"

"Look," I tell Sam, "if we go along with the show, we can keep looking for the thief. And if we find out who it is before the show, we don't have to be in it."

"So we let Mrs. Rushka and everyone else down?"

"We don't have a choice." I can't believe I'm actually fighting to stay in the ballet class. It's not like this is FUN for me. I'm the one having to dress up as a girly girl and pretend I love pink and glitter and strawberry lip gloss all day long! Sam doesn't have to pretend to be a girly girl except when she's in the dance class—and now she doesn't even have to do that because she's playing the *prince*!

Sam thinks for a second. "No, you're right." She tugs off her hair band and shoves it into her bag. "We've got to keep going for now. Like you said, maybe we can catch the thief before the show and then Ayesha and Jeannie can take our places. They'd love that. Let's go see if the CCTV footage is in the basement—maybe that will give us some evidence. Now's the best time, actually, because I saw —"

My tracking device alert bleeps. "Hang on." I pull it out of my bag. I've set it to go off any time that Mr. Jones goes near the soccer exhibit.

"Mr. Jones is by the soccer gear again," I tell Sam, looking at the little tracking light.

"But the CCTV —" Sam starts.

"We can do that after I've seen what he's up to. He's our likeliest candidate at the moment, so I'm going to keep on his tail. If you don't want to stick with me, don't."

Sam flinches. I guess I sounded harsher than I meant to, but I'm getting fed up with her always telling me what I should be doing. And not realizing that I'm on the right track.

My tracker device bleeps again.

I look down and see that he's almost at the memorabilia cabinet. "Why don't I meet you in reception after I check out what he's doing?"

"Right," she says, her voice cold.

She leaves the room without saying another word. I push my way out of the changing rooms and walk as fast as I can towards reception. It's not my fault Sam isn't as suspicious of Mr. Jones as I am. I can't let that stand in the way of catching the thief, especially with the clock ticking.

I run through the main doors and, sure enough, Mr. Jones is in front of the glass case. I bet he's adding up the value of Pelé's trainers in his head. As I come closer, I see him examining the lock at the door edge—probably trying to work out how best to break it. He must catch sight of

my reflection in the glass because he turns towards me as soon as I come up. "Josie. Nice to see you again. Do you have those forms for me yet?"

"Uh, no. Actually, I don't know whether I can do the meet," I say. "I'm going to be really busy rehearsing for the dance show I'm in." The one good thing about being cast as the lead is that I've got a new excuse to give to Mr. Jones.

"Oh dear, how disappointing," he says. "Well, let's see what can be done, shall we? I'd hate you to miss out." He smiles his flashy toothpaste ad smile. "And do try to get those forms for me, all right? Just in case."

He really wants me to do this gala, that's for sure. It makes me nervous the way he stares at me, though. Like he's a magnifying glass and I'm an ant. I'm supposed to be keeping an eye on him, not the other way around!

"Well, I'd better get going, but we'll sort out the swim meet, don't worry." He heads off towards the door and waves at the receptionist.

"See you later, Stella."

The receptionist waves back. "Have a nice day off on Friday, Mr. Jones!"

A day off? I *knew* I did the right thing following him—now I'll be able to search his office while he's away. I turn towards the cabinet so they don't see me smile.

While I'm waiting for Sam, the two janitors walk in and up to the reception desk. "Found a necklace in the changing rooms," says the man I sent off to clean up imaginary strawberry milk. "Must be worth a lot, it's got a 24 karat stamp on it. Can you keep it safe until it's claimed?"

"Of course," the receptionist tells him. "You are good, you two. Honest as ever."

"Oh I could never steal anything," says the woman cleaner. "Could never live with myself if I did something like that."

"That's right," says the man, nodding. "Even if it could get me out of cleaning toilets." They all laugh and then the cleaners go off toward the offices upstairs.

That's two more suspects knocked out then. Everything is still pointing to Mr. Jones.

A minute later, Sam appears at my elbow. "I've done it," she whispers. She's smiling too. I guess she's not mad any more.

"What?"

"Copied the hard drive with the Copycat Clone!" She drags me by the arm through reception and outside. She looks over her shoulder.

"You have?" I can't believe it. Sam's done a huge part of our mission without me.

"I'll tell you about it when we're back at your house," she says.

"I should have come with you. Sorry." But I don't feel sorry; I feel annoyed. I should have been there!

Sam grins. "We've made a real breakthrough—and maybe it will show us Mr. Jones breaking the cameras."

I can't believe I didn't think of that first! This really is a breakthrough. This is going to prove that I've been right all along.

Chapter 9

When we get back, Dad's dancing about the living room with a new gadget from HQ. "Look, isn't it great?" He holds up a small silver hoop between his thumb and forefinger.

I squint. "What is it?"

"It's *genius* is what it is!" Dad clips the hoop to his ear and then presses it. "Zelia, can you hear me?"

Mom comes through from the kitchen, carrying a bunch of papers covered with scribbles. She must be decoding again. "You're showing them the Ring-a-ring?"

Dad nods happily and takes the thing out of his ear.

"A Ring-a-ring?" Sam steps forward to see.

Dad opens his palm and shows us the tiny button on the back of the silver earring. "You press once to call the other number, press again to hang up."

"So it's a bit like a walkie-talkie," I say. "But really small."

"You mean really *genius*." Dad puts the Ring-a-ring phone away in a slim black case. He sighs happily. "I love my work."

"Can we actually *get* to work then?" I want to upload the CCTV footage and prove that Mr. Jones must be the thief!

Once Mom and Dad understand we've got the security footage, they're really pleased. That is, until they find out that Sam got hold of it on her own.

"I don't like the idea of you not sticking together," Mom says, pursing her lips.

Sam turns a bit pink. "I'm sorry. But I saw the staff register over the receptionist's shoulder this morning and saw that there was hardly anything going on right after our class. It was a really good opportunity to nip down to the basement without being seen . . ."

"You didn't tell me about the staff register," I say.

"I *tried* to," Sam says, glaring at me.

I glare back. Maybe she did—but she didn't try *that* hard.

"Well, you should have been with Sam anyway," Mom says to me, "instead of messing around doing whatever you were doing."

Messing around! I was gathering vital spy information! I keep my mouth shut, though. Once we've seen Mr. Jones on the CCTV footage, *that* will be the time to tell them about all my evidence.

In Mission Control, Dad takes Sam's Copycat Clone tail and loads the CCTV files on one of the screens in the wall. The screen splits to show the different areas covered by the cameras, all of it dark

and grainy. Dad gives us each a square to concentrate on. "Look out for 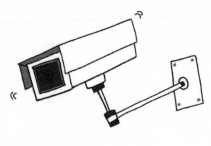 anything out of the ordinary and tell me when to pause," he says as he presses fast-forward.

I scan the footage in my square, crossing my fingers for a sight of Mr. Jones.

"Wait! Look there!" I point at a figure emerging from the corridor that leads to the changing rooms.

I hold my breath as Dad resumes normal speed and we all lean in towards the screen. But straightaway I can see that the figure isn't tall—nowhere near Mr. Jones's height. My stomach plummets with disappointment. When the figure turns towards the camera, we can see that the person is wearing a white theatrical mask and a long cloak.

"What a weird outfit," Sam says.

"Or a clever one," Mom says. "You can't see their face or their body shape, just their height."

The figure advances. A hand reaches up and something covers the screen. It's as if the lens just got covered with ice.

"What happened?" Sam asks.

As we watch, the other screens go gray.

"They sprayed the camera lens before they got in close to it," Dad says. "It's a classic move. You spray the CCTV screen with something like hair spray—it's clear enough that it won't show up if you look at the camera, but it still does what you want it to—covers up what's going on. If you're lucky, it won't be discovered for a while."

"So we still don't know who our thief is," Sam says. "But we have an idea of who it *isn't*." She glances at me but I look away, at the screen, willing it to clear.

I can't believe it—I was so sure Mr. Jones was up to something. And with the cleaners out of the picture and Sam having discovered that the receptionist hates traveling abroad and hasn't even got an up-to-date passport, we're running out of possibilities. My only hope is that when I search Mr. Jones's office, there'll be something to prove it could still be him.

"You really need to figure out who was wearing that cloak," Dad says. "But time's running out."

Thanks, Dad.

I've been so distracted by the film and trying to figure out how that short figure could actually be Mr. Jones (maybe he was walking on his knees?) that I forget all about the show until we arrive at the studio for the next lesson. Mrs. Rushka is full of it, though. "I want the audience to be laughing, clapping, having a wonderful time!"

Unlike the cast of the show.

We spend most of the lesson doing weird jumps called *pas de chats*. It means cat steps apparently. What's next—mouse runs? Donkey jumps? Guinea pig skips? Still, doing cat steps (really badly) means I find out the reason why I've been chosen as the leading lady. It turns out that I'm supposed to be the comic centerpiece for the show.

"I want you to help people have fun!" Mrs. Rushka tells me as I pick myself up off the floor. "So

don't worry if you fall over, Josie—I *want* you to fall over! You will be the comedy star of the night."

In other words, Mrs. Rushka wants me to dance like a doofus.

Of course everyone else in the class is delighted, and Jeannie even smiles at me, figuring her chance to show off is probably better now that I'm going to look like a complete clown next to her.

The whole thing is topped off when we finish the lesson and bump into the girly girl gang outside on their way to go swimming and Melissa tells us that they *can't wait* to see us on stage.

There's only one way to get out of this show. I have got to find the thief!

On Friday morning, we get another Tamper Tester alert. We've had a few of these from the exhibition case, but so far they've turned out to be the cleaners giving the cabinet a good polish or Mrs. Rushka knocking into the glass on her way to class. This one turns out to be the receptionist putting a cup of tea on top of the cabinet. We've still got no evidence. So all through our next ballet lesson, I can only think about being able to search Mr. Jones's room. It's hard to concentrate on a flamingo-shaking-a-fly-off-its-foot move when you're planning to break into an office. In the changing rooms, I tell Sam about my plan.

"Why? It's obvious that it wasn't him tampering with the cameras," Sam says.

"I still think he's up to something," I say.

"Well, I think it's a waste of time." Sam stuffs her tutu into her bag and zips it up. "And we're supposed to be working as a team, remember?"

"You can talk! You're the one who went off and copied the footage on your own!"

"Only because you won't do anything except follow Mr. Jones around! We should be looking at all the possibilities, not just one. Especially now that we've seen he wasn't the one who disabled the cameras."

"But it's stupid to write him off before we're completely sure it's not him." Okay, the figure in the film wasn't Mr. Jones but he *has* still been acting suspiciously!

Sam stares at me. "Are you calling me stupid?"

"No!" I suppose that *is* what it sounded like, but it's not what I meant. Not really.

"You're not interested in what I think, are you?" she asks.

"You're just angry because I don't agree with everything you say. Just because you're good at some spy skills doesn't mean you get to be in charge of our mission."

Sam's eyes bore into me like the level-five monster in the *Dark Destroyer* game on my phone. "No, I just don't like you putting yourself in danger by risking your cover with Mr. Jones. And not ever listening to *my* ideas about who the suspects are."

I glare at her. "Okay. If you're so unhappy, why don't we work alone?"

Sam blinks hard, her eyes shiny. "Fine." She swings round and slams out of the changing rooms.

Good. I've been wanting to work on my own for ages. No more being bossed around. No more being ignored. No more coming second. I'll be like Dan McGuire—a one-boy team.

So why do I feel like rubbish?

Chapter 10

I get up to Mr. Jones's office without anyone seeing me, but once I'm there I realize there is one big problem with working on your own.

You're *on your own*.

There's no one to keep a look out while I'm using the multi-lock spy keys to open Mr. Jones's office door. It doesn't help that I keep thinking about Mr. Jones's habit of sneaking up without me hearing him. Even though I've checked the Sniffer

Dog app on the phone and seen that he's well out of range of the center, my heart feels like it's trying to escape from my chest via my throat. I have to do three checks up and down the corridor before I have the nerve to go ahead. Luckily the spy keys work in seconds. I slip inside and silently close the door behind me. First, I take out a sound detector from my bag and stick it to the door. It will pick up anyone approaching the office from the corridor and bleep to alert me.

I start by rifling through the papers on Mr. Jones's desk. There's a three-day-old edition of the *Bothen Hill News* and a large planner. I flick through the pages and see that all the entries have to do with swimming lessons and staff meetings. I check the drawers and find a selection of swim goggles, a couple of nose clips, and a stopwatch. There's a pile of swimming team registration forms too. I flick through them and notice that they're all much simpler than the one Mr. Jones gave me, which is a bit weird, but there's nothing linking Mr. Jones to the planned theft of the soccer memorabilia exhibition.

It's not like I was expecting him to leave a detailed plan lying around with a confession written on it. But I thought there'd be *something*.

The sound detector on the door bleeps. I rush over to grab it and shove it into my bag. I check my phone. Mr. Jones is still not showing up on Sniffer Dog—it's definitely not him. Whoever it is must just be walking by. If I keep completely silent, no one will guess I'm here. Except . . . there's the sound of a key in the door—someone's opening it! I press myself up behind the door as it swings open. If they come in and let the door close behind them, I'm finished! I hold my breath.

There's a rattle and a clonk of plastic. I can see the edge of a bucket at the door, and hear a man's voice mutter, "Typical. Sonia forgot to put the dusters in the trolley again." There's another rattle as the bucket's picked up, then the door closes as the person retreats. I say a silent thank you to Sonia for forgetting the dusters—she's the only reason the cleaner didn't catch me red-handed.

I wait, in my head counting the thirty seconds I know it takes to walk down the hallway (nice spy tip, Mom), until I'm sure the coast is clear. I crack the door open and stick my head out. No one. I look up and down the hallway and then make a run for it, almost tripping over the latest fruit-patterned, long flowing dress Dad made me wear. It's bad enough that I didn't find anything useful, let alone the fact I almost got caught.

Going at it alone is harder than I thought.

Over the weekend I keep thinking about my argument with Sam and how sure I was that Mr. Jones was the suspect—and how I was completely wrong. And it's weird not having Sam around to hang out and play soccer with. Luckily, Mom and Dad are busy with their own spy work and they believe me when I tell them Sam's spending time with her mom. I'm not ready to tell them about our argument yet. I can't help wondering what I'm going to do if we don't sort things out. That's the problem with working as a team—you get used to it.

I come downstairs on Sunday afternoon and find Mom and Dad sitting in the kitchen over cups of tea and a pile of top-secret documents. I still remember the days when it was just tea and cookies. They're both looking a bit grim. Has Sam called and told them about our fight?

"What's wrong?" I ask.

Mom sighs. "We have an extra problem with your mission, as well as the ticking clock."

Dad gestures at me to sit down. "HQ says it looks as though we have an enemy spy on our heels." He pushes a cookie over to me.

Yeah, like a snickerdoodle is going to fix it, Dad.

For a second the relief of them not knowing about my fight with Sam makes me not take in what they're saying.

"HQ has been monitoring the enemy spies that have been after us," Mom goes on. "They think one of them is in the area and that we might be being watched to see if we are who we say we are."

"HQ doesn't want us to stop trying to find the thief, do they?" Even if it's not going well, I don't want to lose my first ever proper mission!

"No," Dad says. "This is the kind of thing we've been expecting to happen—on a mission or not. Remember, they've been looking for us for some time, so it's possible they've figured out that we may have taken drastic action with our covers."

"You mean, it's possible they've figured out you've forced me to dress up as a girl," I say, folding my arms across my chest and glaring at them. I like to remind them every now and then what they've done to me. In case they've forgotten that asking me to dress up as a girl is a COMPLETE OUTRAGE TO BOYKIND.

"Yes, yes," Mom snaps, in her that's-enough-of-that voice. I can't imagine any enemy spy answering back to my mom when she's using that voice. It sounds like nail clippers.

"So it's even more vital you keep to your cover," Dad says. "I'm thinking maybe we should get some extra hair clips in."

"Dad! Sparkly bunny hair clips aren't going to keep me from being discovered! They don't make me look like a girl—they make me look like an idiot."

"But it *is* important that you remember your backstory," says Mom. "One slip and we could be in real danger."

"I know, I know," I say. I break a cookie into pieces and put one in my mouth to stop myself from confessing to them that I've already slipped. Why did I tell Mr. Jones I used to swim?! I won't be tailing him now because he's definitely *not* the thief, but he'll be on my case all the time trying to get me to swim in the stupid meet. Which could lead the enemy spies right to us.

Sam was right. Not sticking to my cover *was* dangerous.

I decide that tomorrow I'll make sure I avoid Mr. Jones or find a way to get the swim meet problem sorted once and for all.

And say sorry to Sam.

And catch the real thief.

Piece of cake.

Chapter 11

On Monday morning, Sam leaves a message with Mom and Dad saying she'll make her own way to the community center. She obviously doesn't want to spend more time with me than she absolutely has to, not even on the bus. So she's seriously angry with me. Perfect. Walking down from the bus stop, my stomach feels like it's full of bad-tempered jumping beans. I've got to solve all my problems—fast.

I use the Sniffer Dog app to keep a tab on Mr. Jones as I approach the community center, and when I see that he's in the corridor next to Studio Six, I duck into the bathroom (and even remember to choose the girls' room) before he can see me. Problem one avoided.

Now it's time to try to make things right with Sam.

But I don't get the chance to speak to her before the lesson because she's already changed and in the studio when I arrive. She doesn't even glance at me when I come in.

As I go over to the barre, Mrs. Rushka advances on me and grabs me by the arm. "Ah, our leading lady, at last! Come with me, I need to get my leads fitted for costumes. Everyone else, please begin practicing your *pas de chats!*" She starts to pull me forward. I lean back on my heels.

"What's the matter, Josie?" Mrs. Rushka looks over at me, frowning.

"I can't do the fitting."

"Why?" Mrs. Rushka asks.

"Because I . . . don't feel very well," I say. It's true, I don't. This is exactly the kind of situation I need to avoid!

Sam's moved next to Mrs. Rushka but her face is stony. My friend has turned into a rock. Even when Sam first realized I was a boy, she still saved me from being found out at school. Is she really so angry with me that she's not going to help me keep my cover?

Mrs. Rushka puts her hand on my forehead. "You haven't got a fever."

"It's . . . my stomach," I tell her. "It hurts."

"Don't worry, all you have to do for the fitting is stand still and look pretty." Mrs. Rushka smiles. She gives my arm a firm tug so that I'm forced to follow her and gestures for Sam to come too.

How am I going to get out of *this*?

Mrs. Rushka leads me through the studio and into a storeroom. It's enormous, and as we walk in, I spot another smaller door on the other side. I realize that it's one of the fire escapes that we've seen in our 3D model of the center and identified as a possible escape route for the thief.

Mrs. Rushka propels me towards a rack hung with costumes.

"You see? It's perfect." Mrs. Rushka is holding out what has to be the Ugliest Dress in the World. It's made of stiff, shiny material with neon green and red stripes with a big bit of lacy stuff round the neck and wrists.

I'm wondering if Mrs. Rushka actually hates me.

"I'm going to look like a traffic light." Even Dad wouldn't make me wear something this disgusting—and that's saying something.

"We need all eyes to be on you, Josie," Mrs. Rushka says. "I want the attention focused firmly on the stage during the end-of-show finale. It's going to be big, dramatic, and very, very loud. The perfect send-off for me."

It's not just what she says that rings an alarm bell, it's the way she says it. "Send-off? Are you going somewhere, Mrs. Rushka?" I put on my best girly girl smile.

Mrs. Rushka waves her hand as if brushing away a small, annoying, buzzy fly. "Yes, yes, I'm going on holiday straight after the show."

"Oh, where are you going?" Sam takes a step forward. She's got *her* best girly girl smile on too.

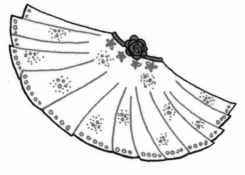

I have a feeling it's better than mine—but I don't mind her beating me on this one.

"Somewhere hot and sunny," Mrs. Rushka says.

Like *Spain*, maybe. I look over at Sam and can see she's thinking the same thing.

"Now, Josie, chop, chop. Let's see what the dress looks like on you. Pop off your tutu and slip it on."

"No!" I take a step backwards.

"What is *wrong* with you, Josie?"

Mrs. Rushka frowns and comes closer, still holding out the dress.

"She's really shy, Mrs. Rushka," Sam says, moving in front of me before Mrs. Rushka can get any closer. She leans towards Mrs. Rushka and whispers in her ear for a long time. I only hear the odd word—"terrified," "sensitive," and "cries."

"Oh dear." Mrs. Rushka tilts her head sympathetically. "You poor thing, Josie." She puts the dress over the top of the rack. "Don't worry, your secret is safe with me. I'll leave you here and you get changed in your own time. I'll wait in the studio while Sam guards the door for you." She pats my arm. "You're lucky to have such a good friend."

"Uh-huh," I say, waiting until Mrs. Rushka has gone out of the door before wheeling round to Sam. "What *exactly* did you tell her?"

Sam smiles. "I just said you have a really nasty rash—all over your body—and that's why you don't like to get changed in front of anyone."

"What about 'sensitive' and 'cries'?"

"I had to make her believe you'd get hysterical if she stuck around—I didn't want her to think you'll be okay making quick changes behind the set in the show." Sam looks like she's on the verge of laughing and saying something jokey about it—then she remembers that she's angry with me. She turns away. "You'd better get that dress on, anyway."

I don't know why I always have to be put in The Most Embarrassing Position Possible.

Every. Single. Time.

Mind you, Sam did just stop me from getting discovered. I pull off my tutu, put the traffic light dress on over my head, and yank it down. "Thanks for getting me out of stripping in front of Mrs. Rushka," I say.

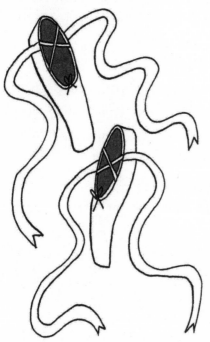

"It's okay." Sam is sounding colder by the second. She's examining a dark purple sequin dress that I know she'd rather throw up on than wear. She's obviously *really* angry.

I hate that she's angry with me.

"You can turn round now," I tell her.

Sam turns, her face set. Then she sees me.

"Oh." Her lips twitch. She puts her hand up to her mouth.

"How bad is it?" I look down. Yeah, I guess it's pretty bad.

Sam bends over as if her stomach hurts. "It's . . . it's . . ." She looks up at me, tears streaming down her face. But she's not crying—she's laughing. "DISGUSTING!"

And I can't help it—I start laughing too. "Thanks, thanks a lot."

"Sorry, but I . . . can't . . . help . . . it," Sam says, as she tries to stop laughing.

This is my chance to put things right.

"Look, I'm really sorry," I tell her. "You were right. I shouldn't have changed my cover story." I explain about the enemy spies that might be watching us.

Sam's face creases up with concern. "That's terrible! You must be really worried." She pauses for a second. "Look, I'm sorry for bossing you around," she says. "I didn't mean to. And I don't want to work alone."

"Neither do I," I say. "I nearly got caught by the cleaner when I searched Mr. Jones's office."

Sam ducks her head and gives me a half smile. "It was tricky when I copied the hard drive too—I bumped into a fitness instructor on the way up from the basement and had to pretend I was lost."

"You didn't tell us that!"

Sam shrugs. "I thought if your mom and dad knew what a near miss it had been, they might have been angrier at you for not coming with me."

I'm starting to realize how mean I've been. "Sorry."

She snorts. "It's fine—seeing you in that dress makes up for everything."

"Yeah, all right. Just wait until you get *your* dress on."

"I'm not playing a girl, though, am I?" Sam gives me her best girly girl smile. "I'm the leading *man*, so I get to wear the trousers."

"Don't rub it in."

Sam makes a zipping gesture across her mouth. "I won't laugh any more. Promise."

I pause. I guess I should tell her everything while we're owning up to things. "I've . . . been a bit jealous about you being a better spy than I am."

Sam's eyes widen. "You're joking! It was your idea to put a Tamper Tester on the CCTV camera! And okay, maybe you changed your cover with Mr. Jones, but you still had the guts to go and investigate him without any help. I wanted to plant a tracking device on Mrs. Rushka the other day but I didn't dare do it without you. And I only went and copied the CCTV film on my own because I knew no one would be around."

"You did the best in the memory tests, though."

"And you're brilliant with the gadgets." She looks at me. "We're *both* good spies—but no one can do everything."

I grin. "Better as a team, then."

"Yeah." She points at my dress. "Though you'll always be better at looking ridiculous."

I sigh. Sometimes you have to let friends make fun of you when you've only just made up.

Chapter 12

The first proper rehearsal for the show the next day reminds me of Dan McGuire in *Dan McGuire and the Brain Drainer of Dubai* when an evil scientist gives him a drug that makes him only half aware of what's going on. That's exactly how I feel. Like I'm floating above myself dressed as a traffic light and looking down, wondering how it happened.

In the warm-up, Mrs. Rushka makes us do endless *pliés* (toad squats), bending down low to the ground and then up again. Ballet discovers the muscles other sports leave out. I can't believe I used to think it was going to be easy!

Then we're on to the main part of the show. Most of it is stuff we've been doing in the lessons, but Mrs. Rushka gets me to act out a "lost princess" routine where Sam comes and saves me. Sam's outfit, of course, is trousers and a coat with brass buckles. Next to me and my eye-wateringly ugly dress, she looks practically normal. Our scene features me doing a lot of flamingo, toad, and beach ball moves ON MY OWN in the MIDDLE OF THE STAGE before Sam comes on and "rescues" me by doing a deer-with-tail-on-fire leap and lots of flamingo spins around me, while I stand on my toes doing beach ball arms. The rest of the class doesn't just laugh, they completely lose control of their senses. Ayesha is laughing so hard that she actually falls over. Jeannie keeps snorting and squealing like a pig on a pig farm. Mrs. Rushka claps with delight. "Lovely, lovely, the audience will love this!"

What she means is, the audience will laugh their heads off. At me.

It's worse than a *month* of Melissa's pamper parties. I have to remind myself that it's all worth it because Sam and I are going to save famous soccer players' sneakers.

Before we rehearse the finale, Mrs. Rushka gathers us all round and raises her hands to get us to be quiet. "The end of the show must be spectacular," she says. "Something to get the audience on their feet, clapping and cheering. So in a moment, we will begin to rehearse a rather different ballet piece that has lots of jumps and stomps," she says. "The important thing is that it is lovely and loud."

I glance over at Sam who's staring at Mrs. Rushka with a frown. So it's not just me who thinks it's odd that Mrs. Rushka

keeps going on about the finale being loud. I put my hand in the air.

"Yes, Josie?"

"Will you be on stage with us, Miss?"

"Oh, no, no, no," Mrs. Rushka says. "This show is all about *you* and showing off your talents."

"So you'll be in the audience watching us?" I keep on.

"I'll be backstage, so that I can monitor the sound system and so forth," Mrs. Rushka says.

I glance at Sam and know she's thinking the same thing—with everyone dancing on stage, it would be easy for Mrs. Rushka to slip off to where the exhibition is.

As soon as Mrs. Rushka lets us have a break, Sam and I have a meeting in one of the hallways leading down to the smallest of the studios.

"It's looking dodgy, isn't it?" Sam says. "Going away straight after the show, storing all her stuff near a fire escape route . . ."

"And the *really loud* finale," I say.

"Exactly."

"Looks like we've got ourselves a new prime suspect. Time for full-on investigating, then?" I grin at Sam.

"Yeah," Sam says, smiling back at me. "Let's do it."

In the studio, while the rest of the class is still looking at themselves doing flamingo moves in the mirror, Sam asks Mrs. Rushka to go over her prince solo routine with her. I slip over to the side of the room and drop a tracking device into her handbag. Then I realize that Mrs. Rushka's wearing ballet flats and has left her ordinary shoes by the studio wall. Bingo! I sit and pretend to be massaging my leg as I stick another device on the bottom of one of Mrs. Rushka's shoes.

After the lesson, we go to the storeroom to change out of our costumes and leave some extra Eye Spy cameras in there at the same time. Then we make our way to reception to see if Sam can have another chat with her source, the receptionist.

We're just coming up to reception when Mr. Jones suddenly appears in front of us. How did he manage to sneak up on me *again*?! I have *got* to remember to check my phone more often!

"Ah, Josie," Mr. Jones says. "Just the person I wanted to see."

The feeling really isn't mutual, Mr. Jones.

"I'm in a bit of trouble, I'm afraid. Some of our swim team can't make the meet on Friday, so I really need you to be a hero and step in."

I feel relief flood through me. "I won't be able to do it then—that's the same day as the dance show."

Mr. Jones shakes his head. "No, no, that's no problem. The meet is in the morning; the show is in the evening. Plenty of time to rest up in between. I just need you for the first key race."

"But I didn't get my forms filled out," I say. Panic fills my chest like a balloon. He can't *make* me get in that pool, can he?

Mr. Jones smiles. "That's okay, Josie. We can sort all that out later." He leans forward so that I can smell the toothpaste on his breath. "To be honest, I need you to help me out here."

"I really wasn't that good, though," I say.

"Oh, now, now, now, no false modesty, all right?" Mr. Jones pats me on the shoulder. "I know you'll be great."

I look over at Sam. I know she'll think of something.

"Yeah, you'll be great, Josie," Sam says. "Of course you can do it."

What is she talking about?!

Mr. Jones looks a bit surprised that Sam's chipped in but his smile is back in place in an instant. "Excellent. You listen to your friend, Josie." He pulls out a sheet of paper from his pocket. "I'll put you down for the first race—the front crawl at ten-fifteen, okay?"

I open my mouth to protest but Sam reaches out and takes the sheet of paper from Mr. Jones.

"She'll be there," she tells him.

"Great stuff," he says. He turns towards me. "I can't tell you how much I'm looking forward to seeing you swim, Josie," he says. "But I must get off and get the rest of the team sorted out. See you later."

As soon as he's gone, I whip round to face Sam. "What do you think you're doing, telling him I'm going to swim in the meet? Have you lost your mind?"

"No, I've just realized—you *were* right to suspect him, but not as a thief."

"What—" I start, and then catch myself. Everything fits together—the weird questions, the form that was different from all the others, his sneaking up on me the whole time, his insistence on me swimming in the meet. "He's the enemy spy!"

Sam nods. "I think he wants you to swim in the meet to expose you as who—what—you really are."

"Then why did you agree?!"

"Because," she says, grinning, "I have a plan."

Chapter 13

Sam won't say anything more until we're safe in my room.

"The thing is," Sam says, "I'm not sure your mom and dad are going to like my idea. It's a bit risky."

"But could it convince him that I'm definitely not who he thinks I am and keep us safe? Because if I don't swim, he might see that as proof that he's right and then we'd really be in trouble."

Sam nods. "If it works, it will *really* work."

I only have to think for about a second. "Then we should do it. But I thought you didn't like taking risks?"

"You've inspired me," she says, smiling. "But you'll have to do exactly as I say."

I take a deep breath. "Okay," I say. "You tell me the meet plan and I'll tell you my idea for exposing Mrs. Rushka."

"Hang on, we don't know it's definitely her yet. You've got to stop jumping to conclusions."

"And you've got to stop bossing me around," I say.

"I'm not—"

We catch each other's eye and laugh.

"Let's just hear each other out," I say.

"Deal," says Sam.

Half an hour later, we've agreed on the plans and there's only one problem: we're going to need a *lot* more gadgets.

Luckily, Mom and Dad go out on a spy errand before dinner so I can sneak into Mission Control and put in an order to HQ. I've decided it's best not

to tell Mom and Dad until just before we expose Mrs. Rushka. If they knew what Sam and I are planning, I'm not completely sure they'd approve.

Actually, I'm completely sure they wouldn't.

For spies, Mom and Dad's security codes for their computer are hilariously bad. Mind you, I guess they didn't think that their own son might one day hack into it. I only have to check a few basics: son's name, son's birthday, and name of son's first hamster.

They've used them all.

So fifteen minutes in, and I'm putting in an order for a stash of gadgets that will cover every part of our plan.

I just hope HQ delivers them while my parents are out.

Since we planted the tracking device, we've been checking the Sniffer Dog app and the Eye Spy

camera footage to see what Mrs. Rushka's been up to. It's all looking more and more suspicious. Yesterday, she spent ages in front of the soccer memorabilia, and she went through the fire exit from the storeroom *three* times. We're convinced she's checking how long it takes to make an escape.

When Sam and I turn up at the community center on Wednesday, there's a line of people waiting to book their sessions for the gym and swimming so we have to wait for a while to sign in. As we wait, I look up at the video screen hanging over the reception desk. The film shows people doing aqua fit—bouncing up and down like balls in the water, people heaving weights in the gym, and then a dance instructor teaching an adult ballet class. A dance instructor who isn't Mrs. Rushka.

Notice everything, Dad said.

When we get up to the counter, I hand over my plastic membership card to be swiped. "Why isn't Mrs. Rushka teaching the adult ballet class?" I ask the receptionist, nodding towards the screen. "I thought she's been teaching here for ages."

"Mrs. Rushka? No, no, my love, our teacher suddenly retired and a couple of days later Mrs. Rushka came and suggested doing an intensive course for us just for the holidays. Very nice of her, even if it is going to be a nightmare organizing your little show."

Sam moves forward, shooting me a glance. "Why's it going to be a nightmare?"

The receptionist glances over her shoulder to make sure there's no one else listening. "Well, you see, we assumed she'd want the show to be in the main sports hall, where we put on most of our events. But Mrs. Rushka's insisting that it's too hot to have the show on in a hall with no air conditioning. So she's building a little stage outside, right in front of the doors there." The receptionist points straight ahead. "Everyone will have to be out of the building. And of course it means carrying all those chairs . . . It's so much more work than having it in the hall would have been. But apparently no air conditioning is a health and safety issue."

"Oh, I see," Sam says.

A temporary stage in the car park in front of the community center reception will bring everyone outside, away from the exhibition. A temporary stage built where the receptionist is pointing will block reception—and the soccer memorabilia exhibition—from view.

"Oh, I see," I repeat after Sam, raising my eyebrows at her.

I give the receptionist my best smile as she hands me my swipe card and my receipt. She may have called me her "love" but she's still just given us a key bit of spy intelligence.

"Nice work," Sam says, as we walk down to the corridors. "It's all adding up so far."

During the lesson, Mrs. Rushka slips into the storeroom twice. So during our next break, Sam and I sneak into it when no one's looking to see what she's been doing. As we search the room, I nudge the clothes rack and something clatters to the ground. I pick it up and do a double take.

"Sam!" I hiss. With one hand I hold up the theatrical mask I've just picked up from the floor, and with the other, I show her the long black cloak I've noticed hanging from the rack. "Look familiar?"

Sam's eyes light up. "The outfit from the CCTV footage!"

I'm about to say something else when we hear the door being pushed open. I duck under the cloak and hold my breath. Sam covers herself with a vomit-green sequin dress next to me.

The door bangs shut and there's a rustling sound. I lean slightly to my right where there's a gap in the cloth and see Mrs. Rushka pulling out her phone from her bag. She taps at it and then waits.

"It's me," she says. "It's all going as planned. I've checked the timings through the exit we chose. It's going to work perfectly, but we must load up during the finale." She pauses, listening. "Yes, yes, my awful ballerinas will be making plenty of noise, don't you worry. They're all natural elephants—especially my star." She laughs.

Just who is she calling an elephant?
I'm a *flamingo*!

Mrs. Rushka pauses again. "Look. You just make sure you've booked the ferry crossing to Spain—we can't miss that auction. Leave everything else to me. We'll make them pay for not selecting you for the team, don't worry."

I squint through the gap to see Mrs. Rushka kissing into the phone. "Bye, bye, love, talk to you later," she whispers. She ends the call and slips the phone into her bag. "Right then," she says to herself. "Back to the no-hopers...." She pushes open the door and disappears out into the studio.

Sam and I stand up and grin at each other. "We'd better go through the fire exit and go to the studio the front way so she doesn't know we were in here with her," I say. I can't help grinning. We've got a lot to do, but it's great to know we're on the right track this time.

Sam bows. "After you, Princess Elephant. . . ."

Our luck keeps up. When I get back to my house, there's a note on the kitchen table from Mom and Dad.

Have a cheese sandwich and a cookie. Love M&D

"Cheese sandwich" is the family code for "Have to go out on an urgent mission" and "cookie" is code for "Will return before dark" but I decide there's no harm in following the instructions anyway. As I'm drying up my plate, the doorbell rings.

Outside there's a man in dark blue overalls with a large box. There's a small red cross on the bottom corner—it's from HQ.

"Delivery." He looks a bit doubtful when he sees I'm not a grown-up.

"Must be something for my mom," I say, reaching out for it.

"Oh. Right, yes." The man nods and hands it over and disappears into his black van.

After checking everything I ordered is there, I race upstairs with the box and shove it under my bed. I've left a note telling Mom and Dad that Sam and I know who the thief is and that we'll have a meeting before the show to update them. But I'm going to sneak out first thing on Friday morning so that Sam and I can carry out the bit of the plan I don't think they'll be so keen on.

If everything goes well, by the end of Friday Sam and I will have put the enemy spy off our trail and revealed the thief of the memorabilia red-handed. If everything goes wrong, by the end of the day my cover will be blown and my family put in danger, and a thief will have made off with one of the most valuable soccer memorabilia collections ever put together.

No pressure, then.

Chapter 14

Thursday's rehearsal goes smoothly, and Thursday night Sam and I go over every last detail of the plan. On Friday morning, my stomach feels like it's full of frogs doing somersaults. But I can't wait to get going. When we get off the bus, Sam and I head up a small side road that leads us round to the back of the community center.

"So, ready to put the first part of Operation Ambitious into action?" She's bouncing on the balls of her sneakers like she's about to take off into a run.

"You're sure it's going to work?"

"As long as we don't mess it up," Sam says cheerfully.

"That's really reassuring, thanks," I tell her. But the grin she gives me does make me feel a bit less nervous.

Only a bit, though. After all, we're about to try to out-spy a real spy.

Our Sniffer Dog apps show us that Mrs. Rushka is round the front of the center, probably supervising the stage being put together, and Mr. Jones is in the swimming pool area— probably waiting for me. So, as per our plan, Sam avoids being seen by going through the set of fire exit doors at the back. The 3D model is really coming in handy for this mission. She's armed with the Ice It freeze

spray I ordered from HQ to disable the alarm for the door.

I walk round to the front. My job now is to make sure Mrs. Rushka is nowhere near the meet. I don't have to go far. She's outside, stapling reams of black cloth to the wooden stage that's gone up in front of the doors. When her back is to me, I take a few photographs on my phone. I think we have everything we need for later, but the more research I do, the better prepared we can be.

I check my watch and then make my way up to the swimming pool and through the glass doors. Mr. Jones is standing in the little area between the pool and the long hallway that leads to the locker rooms.

"Josie! So glad you made it!" Mr. Jones grabs my hand to shake it. "You're looking a bit nervous. You're not thinking of backing out, I hope?" He uses the excuse of shaking my hand to lean down and peer into my face. He's looking for signs of panic—or signs of boy. And let's face it, if I was *really* about to get changed and try to swim in the meet as a *girl*, he *would* see signs of panic. In fact, he'd see nothing BUT panic. Instead, I just smile.

"Back out? Of course not! I'm really looking forward to it."

"Oh." Mr. Jones looks deflated. "Well . . . That's great, then."

"Yes," I tell him. "I can't wait." I reach into my bag and hold up a dark pink swimming costume.

"See?" I can feel Mr. Jones's eyes watching me as I walk down the hallway towards the girls' locker rooms. I bet he's expecting me to run away at the last minute. I turn round before I go in and wave. He immediately drops to the floor and pretends to fiddle with his shoelaces.

Even I noticed he's wearing Velcro trainers.

I smile to myself—I've finally got the hang of it. Dad's right: it *is* all about the details.

I take a deep breath and push my way into the changing rooms.

Sam's assured me that there
are plenty of stalls so I won't
be caught out like when I had to
change in the communal locker room at school.
It's vital to our plan that there *are* stalls. I count
three stalls along and tap twice. Sam swings the
door open and I squeeze inside. She's already
changed into her swimsuit that's identical to the
one I've just shown Mr. Jones.

She pulls on my old wig that we've given a new
Josie-style hedgehog haircut and I help her add the
swimming cap and the large goggles.

"What do you think?" she says.

"Not bad, as long as he's not right up close," I
tell her.

"Okay, so it's your turn," Sam says. She pulls
out a dark brown wig from her bag (another wig!
I'll never be free of them!), pours some water
over it from a flask she's brought to make it look
like I've been swimming, and helps me put it on.
I switch my coat and skirt and let Sam color in
my eyebrows with an eyebrow pencil since Mom
dyed them blond when we first went on the

run. Then Sam hands me a pair of black-framed glasses.

"Perfect," she says, once I've put them on. "No one would ever think you were Josie."

The last thing we do is switch bags. "So you're sure it's going to work?"

Sam smiles shakily. "It's got to, hasn't it?"

I open the stall door. From round the corner I can hear the other swimmers in the gala chatting and laughing as they go through to the pool. As the talking fades away, I draw my head back in and nod—"Go!" Everything banks on Sam going in late—but not too late.

Sam slips out and makes her way to the pool and I go through the locker room door. If the plan backfires, I'm to run over and set off the fire alarm near the exit to create enough confusion for Sam to escape. Let's hope I won't have to.

I take a deep breath and remember what my dad's always said—that people are looking to see what they're expecting to see. *I'm not Josie, I'm not Josie*, I say to myself as I walk up the hall to the pool side. I'm just someone who's been swimming, that's all. I reach up to touch my wet wig to reassure myself.

It works! Mr. Jones looks up, glances at me and then turns towards the pool. I walk briskly towards the bleachers. Mr. Jones scans the swimmers as they line up. I walk up to the second row of spectator seats and slip into a seat at the end of the row.

The front crawl race is announced. Sam takes her place when my name is called out and lines up with the other swimmers, her head down. The tufts of blond hair peeping out from the side of her swimming cap look *exactly* like my dyed hair—from a distance she really does look like me. Or like me if I was, you know, *actually* a girl. For a brief second I picture myself standing there in a bathing suit and shudder. My cover would have been blown quicker than you can say "boys' bits."

Mr. Jones is standing to one side of the pool, staring at Sam. As the lifeguard raises the whistle to her lips, Sam starts coughing violently, completely bending over to her knees. The lifeguard, who's acting as referee, pauses but Sam raises her hand to signal that she's okay and takes her diving position. The referee blows the whistle and the girls dive into the water and start their front crawl. I lean forward and hold my breath as the girls splash past and surge on ahead. Mr. Jones's head follows them too, though I'm pretty sure there's only one swimming cap he's keeping his eye on. What if the cap comes off and pulls the wig with it? What if he gets too close a look at Sam's face when she gets out?

The second hand on the big clock hanging on the wall opposite seems to slow to a standstill as my eyes flick between it and the swimmers. The parents and friends watching erupt into encouraging cheers as the swimmers get closer to the finish. Sam is still with the top few swimmers, though she's not going to win. We decided that while she needed to perform well, it was also important that she didn't come in first so that she didn't get too much attention.

It's not easy, but Sam nails it. She comes up in fourth place, which is perfect—a good position, but nothing that will be particularly noticed. She keeps her head down as she makes her way slowly towards the steps. Mr. Jones moves forward towards them too.

This is the real test.

I get up and very slowly inch my way forward so that I'm just behind him and in earshot. I *have* to know what's going on.

Sam lifts her head as she pulls herself up the last step and onto the pool side and quickly covers herself with a towel. I have to suppress a gasp. It's even better than I expected—her face and upper arms are completely covered with bright red splotches. She looks awful—it's brilliant!

Mr. Jones takes a breath. "Josie?"

Sam coughs. "Allergic!"

"To chlorine?"

Sam nods and coughs again and takes a step towards the locker room.

"So why did you swim?"

"To help—" She coughs again. Then she puts up her hands to her face and staggers off to the locker room.

I slip behind Mr. Jones and through the doors to the hall, and then run full force down to the changing room to meet Sam.

Sam grins when I come into the stall. She's already got her normal clothes on. "Think that went okay, didn't it?"

I pull on my Josie skirt. "I guess we'll know for sure in a minute, but yeah!"

Sam gives me her water bottle so I can get my hair wet and look like I've been swimming.

"What about the rash?" I look at Sam's face and laugh. "I'd better use a bit of that face paint too."

We switch bags and hide away the rest of my disguise clothes. Sam takes out the makeup she'd pinned to her swimsuit strap so she can put a bit on my skin.

"That's good," she says. "It looks like you've got a trace of an allergy but not so much that it looks fake."

"I still don't know how you managed to get it on your face so quickly," I tell Sam. "That fake coughing fit didn't seem to last more than a few seconds."

"Adrenaline," Sam says. "Makes you move really fast. Though it was a bit tricky getting it in and out of the strap of my bathing suit. But you did brilliantly too—you must have had to walk right past Mr. Jones in that disguise!"

"But the next bit is going to be harder."

"Yeah," says Sam. "Now you've got to do a *really* good acting job."

She's right. I have to go and convince a professional spy that my cover is one hundred percent true. My stomach does a flamingo spin all on its own. My legs might not be good at ballet, but my insides have got it down.

Sam leaves ahead of me, going out the same exit as before. Now all that's left for me to do is to go out through reception. As we predicted, Mr. Jones is there, waiting for me. This is it—my chance to prove I'm good enough to be a professional spy. I walk up to him. "Don't you need to be at the pool for the other races?" I ask.

"I just wanted to see if you were okay," he says, peering at my face. "That was quite a reaction."

"Yeah," I say, "it will wear off in an hour or so. I just really didn't want to let you down." I pause and then look at him. "I used to swim a lot but then I became allergic to chlorine and my parents said I shouldn't do it any more. That's why I couldn't fill out those forms—they'd have told me I couldn't do it. But I knew you were desperate for swimmers, and thought I could help you out just this once."

"Just this once," Mr. Jones repeats. He looks deflated, like he's lost something he really wanted. In this case—blowing my cover, and Mom and Dad's.

Tough luck, bozo.

"Yes." I look down, playing the part of being deeply ashamed. "I'm sorry. I should have told you. And I didn't even win the race for you."

Mr. Jones lets out a long, low sigh. "Never mind, Josie. You're not the only one who didn't win today. Another time . . ."

Like never.

"Thanks for being so nice about it,"
I say with the best girly girl smile I've ever
done. "Well, I'd better go—I've got the dance
show to get ready for."

"Yeah, off you go," Mr. Jones says, staring at the
screen over the reception desk, which is showing
a film of an aerobics fitness class. "Break a leg
tonight." He wanders off, looking like he doesn't
know what to do with himself. He's probably not
looking forward to reporting his complete spy
reveal FAIL to his boss.

Operation Ambitious is accomplished. If I could
high-five myself, I would. Instead, I pull out my
phone and send Sam a picture—a thumbs up.

Chapter 15

When Sam and I tell Mom and Dad about the meet at lunchtime, it's safe to say that their first reaction is horror. Actually, so is their second reaction. And their third.

"But why didn't you *tell* us you'd found the enemy spy?" Mom is giving me one of her best laser looks.

"We weren't sure it was him at first," I say. "I thought he might be the memorabilia thief—but I was wrong."

"And then I had this idea of how to get him off your trail but we didn't think you'd approve," Sam says, giving my mom a sheepish look.

"You're right we wouldn't have approved!" Dad pushes his hand through his hair. "No HQ approval, hardly any gadgets . . ."

"Too much *danger*," Mom says, shooting my dad a look.

"Danger, right," Dad says, nodding furiously. "Way too much of that."

"But Sam's plan worked," I say. "It was an awesome plan. And *it worked*."

"There is that, yes," Dad says, still nodding.

"It could have all gone horribly wrong," Mom says. "I don't want you undertaking another plan like that without full disclosure and our approval— do you promise?"

Sam and I look at each other.

"Do. You. Promise?" Mom lasers us both. My mom is sometimes seriously scary.

So then, of course, we have to tell them about our plan for the memorabilia mission—and the stuff I ordered from HQ.

Now Mom's not only got her serious spy look on, she's got her beside-herself-with-rage look on too. "I can't believe you hacked into our computer! You are *never* to do that *ever again*, do you hear?!"

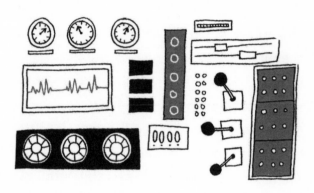

"Though of course, it's good news that you've uncovered the thief in the nick of time," Dad says. "And I've got some magnets that might come in handy."

Mom gives him a look that could scorch an entire forest. Dad coughs. "But we don't approve of you acting without authorization. Not at all."

"And if you ever hack into our computer again—" Mom starts.

"But Josie won't be able to," Sam breaks in. "Because obviously you'll change your passwords to something she can't guess."

"You can bet your bottom I will," says Mom.

I shoot Sam a look. She shrugs as if to say, "She was going to do it, anyway."

And the thought of it clearly calms Mom down. After a bit, she even admits that our plan is quite good.

Which is high praise coming from a super spy like my mum.

We arrive extra early for the dress rehearsal as Sam and I have a lot to set up. The receptionist is about to change over to the one on evening duty so Sam goes off to employ our Distract the Receptionist Plan while I slip the gadgets in place around the stage and scenery. It's easy to hide them because Mrs. Rushka's used endless amounts of black-out material to make sure the backdrop keeps the exhibition completely invisible. As I work, I think about the torture my legs and arms have been through, and the traffic-light dress Mrs. Rushka's forcing me to wear, and about her making me be an *elephant princess* for everyone to laugh at.

I might be an elephant, Mrs. Rushka, but an elephant never forgets.

The afternoon dress rehearsal goes just as we hoped. Thanks to Sam's rash story, I get changed into my vile green-and-red throw-up dress in the staff bathroom so there are no locker room scares. Sam and I have hacked into the music system, so we control the finale music. We simply turn the music up so that it's belted out around the stage.

"Wonderful, everyone, wonderful!" Mrs. Rushka claps her hands together. "I can't wait for tonight!"

Mrs. Rushka clearly thinks that everything is going according to plan.

And it is. It's just not going according to *her* plan.

When the people begin to file in for the show in the late afternoon, I notice that Sam's looking a bit odd.

"Ready?" I ask Sam.

"I forgot something," she says.

I check my watch—we've got about a minute until curtain up. "What is it?"

"I get stage fright," Sam says. She points at her legs—they're shaking.

"You're telling me *now*?"

"I forgot," Sam says.

"You *forgot*?"

"Yes, I *forgot*! We've had quite a lot of important stuff to do, you know," Sam says.

"But do you get it seriously? I mean, are you going to be able to, you know, dance?" I don't know what to say to her! We've got to pull this off or the thief won't be exposed, the exhibition will be gone, and we'll be complete spy failures!

Sam nods but her legs are still impersonating jelly. "I can't do it without you, you know," I tell her. "We're a team." I try to think of the kind of things Mom and Dad have said in the past to encourage me. I reach out and pat her arm. "I'll be proud of you no matter what happens."

Sam snorts and then laughs properly. "Thanks, Josie, a laugh was just what I needed."

Mrs. Rushka is coming into view.

"Good," I say. "Because we're up."

Mrs. Rushka is beaming. "Ready, my lovelies?"

"Ready!" I say. I punch Sam's arm lightly. "Don't worry; it's going to be great."

We take our beginning positions. There are loads of people in the audience—way more than I was expecting—and lots of them are from our school. I see Noah towards the back and recognize Evie from our girls' soccer team sitting near Mom and Dad at the side. Worst of all, the girly girl gang are right in the front row. Melissa's beaming up at the stage, but Nerida and Suzy poke each other in the ribs and laugh when they see me. I can't help shuddering—what if they take photos and show them at school or post them online?

I concentrate on why Sam and I are here— we're doing important spy mission work, just like Dan McGuire. And now we're ready for Operation Showtime.

Sam and I are on the sidelines during the first few routines, but it doesn't feel long at all before it's time for us to take center stage. I take a deep breath and do what I'm supposed to do. I make everyone laugh.

If our little lost princess routine made the dance class laugh before, this time we make everyone hysterical. If I say so myself, my flamingo moves have never been finer.

I might not look exactly like the ballerinas on the film Mrs. Rushka showed us, but my beach ball arms are second to none. The audience is beside themselves and Jeannie looks furious because we've up-staged her. I don't think she's any closer to that television appearance.

And I have to admit it: I'm enjoying myself a lot. I didn't know dancing could be this much fun. I almost forget Sam and I have a job to do.

Almost.

It only seems like seconds before Mrs. Rushka is putting on the music for the finale. Waving to us from the side of the stage, she's got the broadest grin on her face.

"She thinks she's going to get away with it," I whisper to Sam, as we take our places for the last routine. Sam gives me a princely bow in reply and grins. This is when we're expecting Mrs. Rushka to disappear to steal the memorabilia. As the music starts, I do my cat steps but when I glance to the wings of the stage, Mrs. Rushka is still standing there, nodding her head in time to the music. Why hasn't she gone? Has she got someone else to do the theft for her?

I look over at Sam but she's in the middle of a flamingo spin. The next bit of the finale is set at the front of the stage so we'll lose sight of Mrs. Rushka. This is a disaster! If we strike too quickly we won't catch her in the act, but if we leave it too late, she'll escape. I catch Sam's eye as she moves to the front of the stage with Jeannie. She jerks her head towards the side of the stage and mouths "Go!"

I do some cat steps and a flamingo turn. Then I peel off from the rest of the class and do a deer-with-tail-on-fire leap to the back of the stage. It feels like I've jumped a foot in the air, and even over the music I hear the audience gasp. Anyone who thinks ballet is a girly girl thing to do really doesn't know what they're talking about.

I check the wings—Mrs. Rushka has vanished. This is it!

I reach up into a being-a-beach-ball position to the spot in the curtains where I've tucked an extra remote control for the music. Ballet has made me able to stretch up a lot higher than I used to. I hold the remote behind my traffic-light dress and turn the volume up to the max. The idea is to lull Mrs. Rushka into a false sense of security and cover the noise of what we're about to do. The music bellows. I realize I may have gone a bit over the top when I see some people up front covering their ears with their hands.

My flamingo-shaking-a-fly-off move activates the Snip All electronic wire cutter gadget we've stuck to one of the stage trees. On the other side of the stage, Sam turns on the Pull All magnet gadget with some beach-ball arms. The rest of the class stares at us, obviously wondering why we're not doing what we've rehearsed. As soon as we've set off the gadgets, Sam and I usher all the other dancers to the front of the stage and tell them to climb down to where the audience is sitting. They do what we tell them, completely bewildered.

Staples ping out from the curtains onto the stage, and pieces of wire clatter down at the back. The first black curtain tumbles from the wooden frame. Jeannie screams and some people in the audience hold up their phones to start filming as if the show has only just started.

I press the remote control for the music system, turning it off. Immediately, everyone in the front row looks relieved.

The curtains keep collapsing to the ground—and now the gasps begin.

The exhibition area is clearly visible. The glass case where the memorabilia was kept is almost empty—the glass smashed, probably when the music went up to maximum volume. About three quarters of the memorabilia has been packed up. And Mrs. Rushka is right next to the case holding a large, bulging sack. She freezes as the last curtain falls, leaving just the bare wooden supports for the stage.

"She's stealing the soccer memorabilia!" someone shouts from the audience.

"She's behind you!" someone else calls out.

Mrs. Rushka spins around and sprints off down the hallway. We know exactly where she's going.

Sam and I run straight to the outside of the storeroom's fire escape exit. We skid to a stop in

front of it, Sam leaning against the door to keep it closed while I reach under my dress to where I've sewn a pocket for some more Ice It spray. I pull out the can and quickly spray the lock. "That should do it," I tell Sam.

The door shudders as someone on the other side tries to push it open.

"Sorry, Mrs. Rushka," Sam shouts at the door. "That was your last dance!"

I grin at her as I press the Ring-a-ring phone clipped to my ear. "Police?" I say.

"Called," Dad's voice says in my ear. He's right, the Ring-a-ring *is* genius.

By the time the police arrive, we've cleared every spy gadget away and are able to leave the police confused but happy to have caught Mrs. Rushka red-handed.

Really, the only thing that's missing from the evening is a standing ovation.

The following week, Sam's reporter mom writes up the whole thing in the local paper. It turns out that the theft was supposed to be revenge for Mrs. Rushka's husband not having been selected for the Wycombe Wanderers soccer team thirty years prior. Mrs. Rushka figured they'd sell off the memorabilia at the Spanish auction and live off the money she thought her husband should have made from his own soccer career.

"Well, you two," Dad says one morning, "HQ is delighted—and not just about Mrs. Rushka. Apparently, Mr. Jones was looking into several families as part of a preliminary investigation, but because he messed up so much with you, he's been transferred to the enemy spies' catering department. All he'll be doing from now on is making cups of tea." Dad smiles. "So he won't be giving us any more trouble."

"Though we've always got to keep a lookout for new potential threats," Mom says. But even she's smiling.

"And they want you to have these," Dad says. He hands us both a small box.

I open it up. Inside is a silver brooch in the shape of a ballerina. I sigh. "Great."

"Wait," Dad says. "Look a bit closer."

I hold it up and see a series of letters and numbers inscribed along the ballerina's tutu— *NESS 8BD.*

Sam shows me her brooch, which has *EJSS 10* on it.

"That's your official registration code with HQ," Dad tells us. "You've passed your first mission with flying colors—you're officially part of our team."

"So we've been rewarded for good teamwork," Sam says. She raises her eyebrows at me and I laugh.

So, okay, HQ hasn't given the go-ahead for me to be a boy again, but at least I'm another step closer to being a professional spy. And the enemy spies have got to give up at some point. Right?

"Interested in a game of soccer, Josie?" Sam flicks up my soccer into the air and catches it again. "It's been a while."

"Yeah, but I should warn you, I think you'll find my footwork's improved a lot," I tell her.

Half an hour later, I've used two scissor flicks and a flamingo fly-off-the-foot and scored four goals.

You know what?

I've changed my mind.

Ballet is awesome.

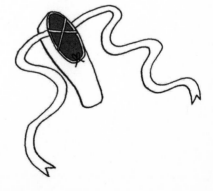

Spies in Disguise

Don't miss:

Boy in Tights

Joe discovers his boring parents are really spies—and that it's up to him to protect their secret identity. There's just one problem . . . He has to pretend to be a girl!